DIAMOND DUST
and Other Stories

Cry, the Peacock

Voices in the City

Bye-Bye, Blackbird

Where Shall We Go This Summer?

Games at Twilight

Clear Light of Day

Village by the Sea

In Custody

Baumgartner's Bombay

Journey to Ithaca

Fasting, Feasting

DIAMOND DUST

and Other Stories

ANITA DESAI

Chatto & Windus
LONDON

Published by Chatto & Windus 2000

2 4 6 8 10 9 7 5 3 1

The following stories have previously appeared elsewhere: 'Diamond Dust' in *New Writing 9*
and 'Five Hours to Simla' in the Spring 1997 issue of *Granta*

First published in Great Britain in 2000 by
Chatto & Windus
Random House, 20 Vauxhall Bridge Road,
London SW1V 2SA

Random House Australia (Pty) Limited
20 Alfred Street, Milsons Point, Sydney,
New South Wales 2061, Australia

Random House New Zealand Limited
18 Poland Road, Glenfield,
Auckland 10, New Zealand

Random House (Pty) Limited
Endulini, 5A Jubilee Road, Parktown 2193, South Africa

The Random House Group Limited Reg. No. 954009
www.randomhouse.co.uk

A CIP catalogue record for this book
is available from the British Library

ISBN 0 7011 6900 1

Papers used by Random House are natural,
recyclable products made from wood grown in sustainable forests.
The manufacturing processes conform to the environmental
regulations of the country of origin

Printed and bound in Great Britain by
Mackays of Chatham plc, Chatham, Kent

Contents

Acknowledgements

Many thanks to the Civitella Ranieri Foundation for providing me with a summer in Umbria where I revised these stories. The author and publisher are grateful to New Directions and Carcanet Press for permission to reproduce the extracts from 'In Uxmal' and 'Exclamation' from *Selected Poems* by Octavio Paz and *The Collected Poems of Octavio Paz, 1957–1987* respectively, quoted on pages 148 and 154 of 'Tepoztlan Tomorrow'.

To My Students at M. I. T.
Who Have Been My Teachers

Diamond Dust
and Other Stories

Royalty

ALL was prepared for the summer exodus: the trunks packed, the household wound down, wound up, ready to be abandoned to three months of withering heat and engulfing dust while its owners withdrew to their retreat in the mountains. The last few days were a little uncomfortable – so many of their clothes already packed away, so many of their books and papers bundled up and ready for the move. The house looked stark, with the silver put away, the vases emptied of flowers, the rugs and carpets rolled up; it was difficult to get through this stretch, delayed by one thing or another – a final visit to the dentist, last instructions to the stockbrokers, a nephew to be entertained on his way to Oxford. It was only the prospect of escape from the blinding heat that already hammered at the closed doors and windows, poured down on the roof and verandas, and withdrawal to the freshness and cool of the mountains which helped them to bear it. Sinking down on veranda chairs to sip lemonade from tall glasses, they sighed, 'Well, we'll soon be out of it.'

In that uncomfortable interlude, a postcard arrived – a cheap, yellow printed postcard that for some reason to do with his age, his generation, Raja still used. Sarla's hands began to tremble: news from Raja. In a quivering voice she asked for her spectacles. Ravi passed them to her and she peered through them to decipher the words as if they were a flight of migrating birds in the distance: Raja was in India, at his ashram in the south, Raja was going to be in Delhi next week, Raja expected to find her there. She *would* be there, wouldn't she? 'You won't desert me?'

After Ravi had made several appeals to her for information, for a sharing of the news, she lifted her face to him, grey and mottled, and said in a broken voice, 'Oh Ravi, Raja has come. He is in the south. He wants to visit us – next week.'

It was only to be expected that Ravi's hands would fall upon the table, fall onto china and silverware, with a crash, making all rattle and jar. Raja was coming! Raja was to be amongst them again!

A great shiver ran through the house like a wind blowing that was not a wind so much as a stream of shining light, shimmering and undulating through the still, shadowy house, a radiant serpent, not without menace, some threat of danger. Whether it liked it or not, the house became the one chosen by Raja for a visitation, a house in waiting.

With her sari wrapped around her shoulders tightly, as if she were cold, Sarla went about unlocking cupboards, taking out sheets, silver, table linen. Her own trunks, and Ravi's, had to be thrown open. What had been put away was taken out again. Ravi sat uncomfortably in the darkened drawing room, watching her go back and forth, his lips thin and tight, but his expression one of helplessness. Sometimes he dared to make things difficult for her, demanding a book or a file he knew was at the very bottom of the trunk, pretending that it was indispensable, but when she performed the difficult task with every expression of weary martyrdom, he relented and asked, 'Are you all right? Sarla?' She refused to answer, her face was clenched in a tightly contained storm of emotion. Despondently, he groaned, 'Oh, aren't we too old –?' Then she turned to look at him, and even spoke: 'What do you mean?' Ravi shook his head helplessly. Was there any need to explain?

Raja arrived on an early morning train. Another sign of his generation: he did not fly when he was in India. Perhaps he had not taken in the fact that one could fly in India too, or else he preferred the trains, no matter how long they took, crawling over the endless, arid plains in the parched heat before the rains. At dawn, no sun yet visible, the sky was already white with heat; crows rose from the dust-laden trees, cawing, then dropped to the ground, sun-struck. Sweepers with great brooms made desultory swipes at the streets, their mouths covered with a strip of turban, or sari, against the dust they raised. Motor rickshaws and taxis were being washed, lovingly, tenderly, by drivers in striped underpants. The city stank of somnolence, of dejection, like sweat-stained clothes. Sarla and Ravi stood on the railway platform, waiting, and when Sarla seemed to waver, Ravi put out a gentlemanly hand to steady her. When she turned her face to him in something like gratitude or pleading, a look passed between them as can only pass between two people married to each other through the droughts and hurricanes of thirty years. Then the train arrived, with a great blowing of triumphant whistles: it had completed its long journey from the south, it had achieved its destination, hadn't it *said* it would? Magnificently, it was a promise kept. Immediately, coolies in red shirts and turbans, with legs like ancient tree roots, sprang at the compartments, leaping onto the steps before the train had even halted or its doors opened, and the families and friends waiting on the platform began to run with the train, waving, calling to the passengers who leaned out of the windows. Sarla and Ravi stood rooted to one place, clinging to each other in order not to be torn apart or pushed aside by the crowd in its excitement.

The pandemonium only grew worse when the doors were unlatched and the passengers began to dismount at the same time as the coolies forced their way in, creating human gridlock. Sighting their friends and relatives, the crowds on the platform began to wave and scream. Till coolies were matched with baggage, passengers with reception parties, utter chaos ruled. Sarla and Ravi peered through it, turning their heads in apprehension. Where was Raja? Only after the united families began to leave, exhorting coolies to bring up the rear with assorted trunks, bedding rolls and baskets balanced on their heads and held against their hips, and the railway platform had emerged from the scramble, did they hear the high-pitched, wavering warble of the voice they recognised: 'Sar-la! Ra-vi! My dears, how *good* of you to come! How *good* to see you! If you only knew what I've beeen through, about the man who insisted on telling me about his *alligator* farm, describing at such length how they are turned into *handbags*, as though I were a *leather merchant . . .*' and they turned to see Raja stepping out of one of the coaches, clutching his silk dhoti with one hand, waving elegantly with the other, a silver lock of his hair rising from his wide forehead as he landed on the platform in his slippered feet. And then the three of them were embracing each other, all at once, and it might have been Oxford, it might have been thirty years ago, it might even have been that lustrous morning in May emerging from dew-drenched meadows and the boat-crowded Isis, with ringing out of the skies and towers above them – bells, bells, bells, bells . . . .

'And then there was *another* extraordinary passenger, a young man with hair like a nest of serpents, you know, and when he understood I would *not* eat a "two-egg mamlet" offered to me by this *incredibly* ragged and *totally* sooty little urchin with a tin tray under his arm, nor even a "*one*-egg mamlet" to please him or anyone, this marvellous person leapt down from the bunk above my head, and shot out of the door – oh, I assure you we were at a standstill, in the most *desolate* little station imaginable, for no reason I could see or guess at if I cudgelled my brains ever so *ferociously* – and then he returned with a basket *overflowing* with fruit, a positive *cornucopia*. Sarla, you'd have *fainted* with bliss! Never did you see such fruit; oh, nowhere, nowhere on those mythical farms of California, certainly, worked on by those armies of the exploited from the sad lands to the south, I assure you, Ravi, such fruit as seemed a reincarnation of the fruit one ate as a child, *stolen*, you know, from the neighbour's orchard, fruit one ate hidden in the *darkest* recesses of one's compound, surreptitiously, one's tongue absolutely *shrivelled* by the *piercing* sweetness of the mangoes, the *cruel* tartness of unripe guavas, the unripe pulp of the plantains. Oh, Sarla, such joys! And I sat peeling a *tiny* banana and eating it – it was no bigger than my little finger and contained the flavour of the ripest, sweetest, best banana anywhere on earth within its cunning little yellow speckled jacket – I asked, naturally, what I owed him. But that

incredible young man, who looked something like a cornucopia *himself*, with that abundant hair — it had such a quality of
liveliness about it, every strand almost *electric* with energy — he
merely folded his hands and said he would not take one paisa
from me, not *one*. *Well*, of course I pushed away the basket
and said I could not possibly accept it, totally against my
principles, etcetera, and he gave me this tender, tender smile,
quite unspeakably loving, and said he could take nothing from
me because in a previous incarnation I had been his
grandfather: he recognised me. "What?" said I, "*what*? What
makes you say so? How *can* you say so?"'

'Watch out!' Ravi shouted at the driver who overtook a
bullock cart so closely he almost ran into its great creaking
wheels and overturned it.

'And he merely smiled, this sweet, *ineffably* sweet smile of
his, and assured me I was no other than this esteemed ancestor
of his who had left his home and family at the age of fifty and
gone off into the Himalayas to live as a hermit and meditate.
"*Well*," said I —'

'Slow down,' Ravi ordered the driver curtly.

'"*Well*," said I, "I *assure* you I have never been in the
Himalayas — although it is *indeed* my life's ambition to do so,
and therefore I could not have returned from there." By the
way, I began to wonder if it was *altogether* flattering to be
called grandfather by a man by no means in the first flush of
youth, more like the becalmed middle years, whereupon he
told me — imagine, Sarla, imagine, Ravi — he told me his
grandfather had *died* there, in Rishikesh, on the banks of the
Ganga, many years ago. His family had all travelled up from
Madras to witness the cremation and carry the ashes to
Benares, but *now*, in the railway carriage, that little tin box
baking in the sun as we crossed the red earth and ravines of

Central India, he claimed he'd seen his reincarnation. He was as *certain* of it as the banana in my hand was a banana! He would not tell me *why*, or *how*, but he was clearly a clairvoyant. And isn't that a *superb* combination: clearly clairvoyant! Or do you think it a touch *de trop*? Hmm, Ravi, Sarla?'

The car lurched around one of the countless circles set within the radiating avenues of New Delhi, now steadily filling with traffic that streamed towards the city's business and government centres, far from this region of immense jamun trees, large low villas, smooth hedges, closed gates, sentries in sentry boxes, and parakeets in flamboyant trees.

'But that is the kind of experience, the kind of encounter that India bestows on one like a *gift*, a *jewel*,' Raja was fluting as the car drew up at one of the closed gates. The driver honked the horn discreetly, the watchman came hurrying to unlock it, and they swept in and up the drive to the porch that stood loaded with the weight of magenta bougainvillea. 'And,' Raja continued as he let the driver help him out of the car, 'I was so *delighted*, so *overjoyed* to find it still so, Ravi, in spite of that frightful man you have installed as the head of your government – an *economist*, is he not? – yes, please, I shall need that bag almost *immediately*, and the other too, if I am to bathe and refresh myself, *but*,' he concluded, triumphantly, 'what further refreshment can one *possibly* require after one has already been blessed with such, such *enchanting* accept-ance, not, not physical, but positively, positively . . .'

'Spiritual?' Ravi ventured, smiling, as he helped Raja up the stairs into the shaded cool of the veranda with its pots of flowers and ferns, a slowly revolving electric fan and an arrangement of wicker furniture where he lowered Raja into an armchair with a flowered cushion.

It was not that Raja was any more elderly than they. They
had all been contemporaries at Oxford, and Raja may even
have been a year or two younger. Sarla had complained that
his southern ancestry had given Raja an unfair advantage over
their northern genes which seemed to produce businessmen
and shopkeepers more readily than mathematicians or philo-
sophers. Yet there was about him an air of fragility, of some
precious commodity that they had been called upon to cherish.
At Oxford Ravi had found himself taking Raja's laundry to be
done while Raja, who had neglected to attend to it till he had
absolutely nothing left to wear, had stayed in bed under his
blankets till Ravi returned with fresh clothes. He was wryly
amused as well as a little annoyed to find that he still fell into
the trap.

Sarla was hurrying into the house, to make sure Raja's
luggage was carried carefully into the room prepared for him
— the bedroom at the back of the house, which Raja loved
because it looked onto a garden full of lemon trees and
jasmine vines that he said he dreamt about during that part of
the year that he spent in Los Angeles — and against Raja's
wishes to order breakfast, because, after all, she and Ravi had
not benefited from the generosity of the young man with hair
like a serpent's nest in the railway carriage, she said a little
acidly.

Why her words sounded acid, she could not say. It was all
she could do not to go down on her knees and remove Raja's
slippers from his feet, or to bring water in a basin and wash
them. She had to sharpen her faculties to fight that urge. But
she brought out the coffee pot herself — she had taken the
silver coffee service out of storage for Raja's visit — and
poured him a cup with all the grace that she had acquired in
her years as a diplomat's wife in the embassies and High
Commissions where Ravi had 'served', she 'presided'. She

could scarcely restrain herself, only tremblingly managed to restrain herself from mentioning that last day in May, that last embrace – oh, it would be so unsuitable, so unsuitable –

And then a second car came sweeping up the drive, parked beside theirs – an identical car, a silver-grey Ambassador with tinted glass and window curtains – and her sister tumbled out of the driver's seat, a woman almost identical to Sarla, and in an equal state of excitement and agitation. And then they *were* all embracing each other, after all, successively, simultaneously.

Maya had not been with them on the bank of the festive, the bacchanalian Isis that May morning; she had not fetched Raja's laundry or cooked him rice on a gas ring on foggy winter nights when he could not walk to the Indian restaurant in the cold, not with his asthmatic condition: Maya had been at the London School of Economics a few years later. Maya had also met her husband at university, but his path had been different from Ravi's. 'No bloody Civil Service for me; I've always thought it most *uncivil*,' Pravin had declared when Maya suggested it, 'and at this stage of history can you really contemplate anything so reactionary? Are we not moving into the future, *free* of colonial institutions?' So it had been a political career for Pravin, not the dirty politics of people Raja had just referred to so disparagingly, but politics as practised by the press, idealistically, morally, scrupulously (even if only on paper). And so, when Maya embraced Raja, it was with vigour, with her head tossed back with pride so that her now grey hair hung from her shoulders with as carefree an air as a young girl might toss her darker, glossier locks, and with a laugh that rang out resonantly. 'What, you've travelled by train in a silk dhoti? Oh Raja, must you go to such *extremes* when you play the the southern gentleman visiting the barbarians of the north?' and Raja hung upon her shoulder and shook his finger at her, fluting at a higher pitch than ever before, 'Is that husband of yours still playing the patriot while dressed in Harris tweeds, and does he still wear that mouldy felt hat when following the elections amongst the cow-dung patties and buffalo sheds of Bihar?' and Sarla was retreating to the wicker sofa with the coffee tray, glowering, turning ashen and tight-lipped once more. But her occupation of the sofa was strategic – now Maya and Raja could not sit upon it, side by side: it belonged to her, and she could preside, icily, silver coffee pot in hand, looking upon the two as if they were somewhat trying children, and Ravi would give her a look – of sympathy, or pity? – from the stool on which he perched, waiting patiently to be passed a cup.

She passed it, then said, interrupting Maya who was giving a humorous account of the last election campaign Pravin had covered, 'If to go to the Himalayas is your life's ambition, Raja, then that can easily be achieved. Won't you consider driving up with us when we go for the summer to *Winhaven?*'

'Winhaven? Winhaven?' Raja twisted around to her. 'Oh, Sarla, Sarla, the very word, the very name – it recalls – how does it go –

"I have desired to go
Where springs not fail –"

and then? And then? How does it go –

"And I have asked to be
Where no storms come
Where the green swell is in the heaven's dumb,
And out of the swing of the sea –"

remember? remember?'

Who did not? Who did not, Sarla would have liked to
know, but suddenly Simba was upon them, bursting out of the
house, his great tail thumping, his claws slithering across the
veranda tiles in his excitement as he dashed at Maya, then at
Ravi, finally at Raja and, to Sarla's horror, Raja was pushed
back into his chair by Simba's vigorous attention, but Raja
was pushing back at him, laughing, 'Oh, Simba, Simba of the
Kenyan highlands! You remember me, do you?' and Sarla,
cupping her chin in her hand, leaving her coffee untouched,
watched as Raja, suddenly as sprightly as a boy, the boy who
had bicycled helter-skelter down the streets of Oxford, dark
hair rising up from his great brow and falling into the
luminous eyes, now ran down the stairs with Simba into the
garden, then bent to pick up a stick and send it flying up at the
morning sun for the pleasure of having Simba leap for it. Old
Simba, usually so gloomy, so lethargic, was now springing up
on his hindlegs to catch the falling toy and run with it into the
shade of the flamboyant tree, Raja following him, his pale silk
dhoti floating about him, his white hair glistening, making the
startled parakeets fly out of the clusters of scarlet flowers with
screams.

Then both Sarla and Maya released small sighs. Ravi
watched their expressions from the stool on which he was
perched, and finally asked, diffidently, 'May I have a lump of
sugar and a little milk, please?'

In spite of his poetic response to Sarla's suggestion that he
accompany them to the mountains, Raja continuously post-
poned the journey. No, he had come to Delhi, all the way to
Delhi in the heat of June, to see them, to relive the
remembered joys of their beautiful home. How could he cut

short his time here? And there was so much for him to see, to do, to catch up on. He wanted Sarla to drive him to the silver market in Chandni Chowk so he could gaze upon the magnificent craftsmanship on display there, perhaps even purchase a piece to take back with him to California where the natives had never seen such art bestowed upon craft, and then if Maya were to accompany him to the Cottage Industries emporium, and help him select a pashmina shawl, then he could be happy even on those chill, rainy days that he was forced to endure. What, didn't they *know*, California had such weather? Had they been deceived by posters of palm trees and golden beaches? Didn't they know the *fraudulence* inherent in the very notion and practice of tourism, that abominable habit of the Western world? Tourism! Now, when *he* returned to India, it was not to see the sights, he already knew them – they were imprinted upon his heart – but to imbibe them, savour them, nourish himself upon them. And so when Sarla and Ravi took him to Nizamuddin and beside the saint's tomb they heard a blind beggar play his lute and sing in a voice so soulful that it melted one's very being,

'When I was born
I was my mother's prince.
When I married
I became my wife's king.
But you have reduced me
To being a beggar, Lord,
Come begging for alms
With my hands outstretched –'

it was as if the thirst of Raja's pilgrim soul was being slaked, and never had thirst been slaked by music so sublime as made by this ancient beggar in his rags, a tin can at his knee for alms – and of course he must have whatever was in Raja's purse, every last coin, alas that they were so few. Now if this beggar were performing in the West, the great theatres of every metropolis would throw open their doors to him. He would perform under floodlights, his name would be on posters, in the papers, on everyone's lips. Gold would pile up at his feet – but then, would he be such a singer as he was now, a pilgrim soul content to sit in the shade of the great saint Nizamuddin's little fretted marble tomb, and dedicate his song to him as homage?

Raja, leaving his slippers at the gateway to the courtyard, approached the tomb with such ecstasy etched upon his noble features that Sarla, and Ravi too, found themselves gazing at him rather than about them – Sarla's bare and Ravi's stockinged feet on the stones, braving the dirt and flies and garbage that had first made them shrink and half turn away. Sarla had held her sari to her nose as they passed a row of butchers' shops on their way to the tomb, buffalo's innards had hung like curtains in the small booths, and the air was rife with raw blood and the thrum of flies, and she asked Raja, in the car, 'How is it that you, a vegetarian, a Brahmin, walked in there and never even twitched your *nose*?' He cast his eyes upon her briefly – and they were still those narrow, horizontal pools of darkness she remembered – and sighed, 'My dear, true souls do not turn away from humanity or, if they do, it is only to meditate and pray, then come back, fortified, to embrace it – beggars, thieves, lepers, whoever – their sores, their rags. They do not flinch from them, for they know these are only the covering, the concealing robes of the soul, don't you know?' and Sarla, and Ravi, seated on either side of

Raja on the comfortably upholstered back seat of the air-conditioned Ambassador, now speeding past the Lodi Gardens to their own green enclave, wondered if Raja was referring to himself or the sufi.

That afternoon, as they sat on the veranda, sipping tea and nibbling at the biscuits the cook had sent up in a temper (he was supposed to be on leave, he was not going to bake fancy cakes at a time when he was rightfully to have had his summer vacation, and so the sahibs could do with biscuits bought in the bazaar), Raja, a little melancholy, a little subdued – which Sarla and Ravi put down to the impression left on him by their visit to the sufi's tomb – piped up in a beseeching voice, 'Sarla, Ravi, where are those ravishing friends of yours I met when you were at the High Commission in London? The Dutta-Rays, was it not? You must know who I mean – you told me how they'd returned to Delhi and built this absolutely fabulous hacienda in Vasant Vihar. Isn't that quite close by?'

'It is,' Ravi admitted.

Like a persistent child, Raja continued, 'Then *why* don't we have them over? This evening? I remember she sang like a nightingale – those melancholy, funereal songs of Tagore's. Wouldn't they be perfect on an evening like this which simply hangs suspended in time, don't you know, as if the dust and heat were holding it in their *cruel* grasp? Oh, Sarla, do telephone, do send for her – tell her I *pine* to hear the sound of her avian voice. Just for that, I'm even willing to put up with her husband who I remember finding – how shall I put it – a *trifle* wanting?'

Sarla found herself quite unwilling. Truth be told, the morning's expedition had left her with a splitting headache; she was not in the habit of walking around in the midday sun, leave that to mad dogs and – she'd always said. Even now, her temples throbbed and perspiration trickled discreetly down the back of her knees, invisible under the fresh cotton sari she'd donned for tea. But Raja would not hear of a refusal, or accept any excuse. If she thought the Dutta-Rays had left for Kashmir, why did she not ring and find out? Oh, there was no need to get up and *go* to the telephone – 'In this land of fantasies fulfilled, isn't there always a willing handmaid, so to speak, to bring the mountain to Mohammed?' and Sarla had to send for the telephone to be brought out to the veranda, the servant Balu unwinding the telephone line all the way, and she was forced to speak into it and verify that the Dutta-Rays were indeed still in Delhi, held up by a visit from a former colleague at India House, but were going out that evening to that party – didn't Sarla and Ravi know of it? 'We're supposed to be *away*,' Sarla said stiffly into the telephone. 'Everyone thinks we are in the *hills* by now. We usually are.' Well, the Dutta-Rays would drop in on their way – and so they did, she a vision of grace in her finely embroidered Lucknow sari, pale green on white, to Raja's great delight, and only too willing to sing for his delectation, only not tonight since they were already late.

So Sarla and Ravi found themselves throwing a party – a party that was to be the setting for a recital given by Ila Dutta-Ray, a woman neither of them had any warm feelings for, remembering how unhelpful she had been when they had first arrived in London and so badly needed help in finding a flat, engaging servants, placing their children in school, all so long ago of course. Instead of *helping*, she had sent them her old cook, declaring he was the best, but really saving herself the air fare back to India because he proved good for nothing but superannuation. They rang up whoever of their circle of friends remained in Delhi to invite them for the occasion. It was quite extraordinary how many friends Raja remembered and managed to trace, and also how many who were on the point of going away, changed their plans on hearing his name and assured Sarla and Ravi they would come.

Then there occurred a dreadful incident: Sarla was choosing from amongst her saris one cool enough for the evening ahead, which was, of course, one of the summer's worst, that kind of still, yellow, lurid evening that it inflicted when one thought one could bear no more, and meant that the recital would be held not in the garden after all but in the air-conditioned drawing room instead, when a terrible thought struck her: she had forgotten to invite Maya! Maya and her husband Pravin! How could she have? It was true Maya had told her Pravin was very preoccupied with a special issue his paper was bringing out on the rise of Hindu fundamentalism but that was no reason to assume they might not be free. Sarla stood in front of the mirror that was attached to one leaf of the armoire, and clasped her hand over her mouth with a look so stricken that Ravi, coming in to ask what glasses should be taken out for the evening, wondered if she had a sudden toothache. 'Ravi! Oh, Ravi,' she wailed.

The telephone was brought to her – Balu unwinding the coils of an endless wire – and the number dialled for her. Then Sarla spoke into it in gasps, but unfortunately she had not taken the time to collect her wits and phrase her invitation with more tact. Maya's sharp ears picked up every indication that her sister had been unforgivably remiss, and coldly rejected the insulting last-minute invitation, insisting proudly that Pravin was working late and she could not possibly leave his side, he never wrote a line without consulting her.

As if that was not agony enough, Sarla had to undergo the

further humiliation of Raja piping up in the middle of the party — just as Ila Dutta-Ray was tuning her tanpura and about to open her mouth and utter the first note of her song — 'But Sarla, where is Maya, that aficionado of Tagore's music? *Surely* we should wait for her? *Why* is she so late?' An awful hush fell — and Sarla again assumed her stricken look. What was she to say, how was she to explain? She found herself stumbling over Maya's insincere excuse, but of course everyone guessed. Frowning in disapproval, Ila Dutta-Ray began her song on a very low, very deep and hoarse note.

In retaliation, Maya and Pravin threw a party as soon as Pravin's column had been written and the special issue had gone to press, and *their* party was in honour of the Minister of Human Resources, whose wife was such an admirer of Raja's, had read every word he had written and wanted so much to meet him — 'in an intimate setting'. Since she had made this special request, they had felt obliged to cut down their guest list — and were sure Sarla and Ravi would not mind since they had the pleasure of Raja's company every day. But when Ravi stoically offered to drive Raja across to their house, he found the whole road lined with cars, many of them chauffeur-driven and with government number plates, and had the humliation of backing out of it after dropping Raja at the gate, then returning to Sarla who had given way to a fierce migraine and was insisting that they book seats on a train to the hills as soon as possible.

'But don't we need to wait till Raja is gone?'

'Raja is incapable of making decisions — we'll have to make his for him,' she snapped, waving at Balu who was slouching in the doorway, waiting to take away the remains of their meagre supper from the dining table.

She was still agonised enough the following morning – digging violently into half a ripe papaya in the blazing light that spilt over the veranda even at that early hour – actually to ask Raja, 'How can you bear this heat? Do you really not mind it? I feel I'm going to collapse –'

Raja, who had a look of sleepy contentment on his face – he had already meditated for an hour in the garden, done his yoga exercises, bathed, drunk his tea and had every reason to look forward to another day – did not seem to catch her meaning at all. Reaching out to stroke her hand, he said, 'I know what you need, my dear – a walk in the sublime Lodi Gardens when the sun is setting and Venus appears in the sky so *silently* –' and went on to describe the ruins, their patina of lichen, their tiles of Persian blue, the echoes that rang beneath their domes, in such terms that Sarla sank back in her chair, sighing, agreeing.

What she did not know was that he had already arranged to walk there with Maya, Ila Dutta-Ray, and the wife of the Minister of Human Resources who, it turned out, had read that book of verses he had written when in Oxford and had published by a small press in London, long expired, so that copies were now collectors' pieces. All three women owned such copies. And Sarla found herself trailing behind them while Raja pranced, actually pranced with delight, with enthusiasm, in their company. At their suggestion he recited these verses:

'The lamp of heaven is hung upon the citrus bough,
The nightingale falls silent.
All is waiting,
For a royal visit by night's own queen –'

and then burst into mocking, self-deprecating laughter, waving away their protests to say, 'Oh, those adolescent excesses! What was I *thinking* of, in Oxford, in the fog and the smog and the cold I suffered from perpetually! Well, you know, I was thinking of – *this*,' and he waved at the walled rose garden and beyond it the pond and beyond that the tombs of the Lodi emperors surrounded by neem trees, and they all gazed with him. Eventually the Minister's wife sighed, 'You make us all see it with new eyes, as if we had never seen it before.'

Sarla, who had hung back, and was standing by a rose bush, fingering the fine petals of one flower pensively, realised that this was so exactly true: it was Raja who opened their eyes, who made them see it as they never saw it themselves, as a place of magic, enchantment, of pleasure so immense and rich that it could never be exhausted. She gazed at his back, his noble head, the silvery hair, the gracefully gesturing arm in its white muslin sleeve, there in the shade of the neem tree, totally disregarding the dust, the smouldering heat at the summer day's end, and seeing it all as romantic, paradisaical – and she clasped her hands together, pressing a petal between them, grateful for knowing him.

That evening she tried again. 'Raja, I *know* you would love Winhaven,' she told him, interrupting the Vedic hymn he was reciting to prove to Ravi that his Sanskrit was still fluent – hadn't he taught it to the golden youth Berkeley, of Stanford, of the universities in Los Angeles and San Francisco, for all these years of his exile? 'And I would love to see you in the Himalayas,' she went on, raising her voice, 'because they would make the most perfect setting for you. Perhaps you would begin to write again over there –'

'But darling Sarla,' Raja beamed at her, showing both the pleasure he took in her suggestion and his determination not to be swept away by it, 'Maya tells me there is to be a lecture at India International Centre next week on the Himalayas as an inspiration for Indian poets through the centuries, and I would *hate* to miss it. It's to be given by Professor Dandavate, that old bore – d'you remember him? What a *dreary* young man he was at Oxford! I can quite imagine how much drearier he is now – and I can't resist the opportunity to pick holes in all he says, and in public too –'

'But next week?' Sarla enquired helplessly. 'It'll – it'll be even hotter.'

'Sarla, don't you *ever* think of anything else?' he reproved her gently, although with a little twitch of impatience about his eyes. 'Now I don't *ever* notice the heat. Drink the delicious fresh lemonades your marvellous cook makes, rest in the afternoons, and there's no reason why you shouldn't *enjoy* the summer. Oh, think of the fruit alone that summer brings us –'

But it was the marvellous cook himself who brought an end to Raja's idyll in Sarla and Ravi's gracious home: that very day he took off his apron, laid down his egg whisk and his market bag, declared that enough was enough, that he was needed in his village to bring in the harvest before the monsoon arrived. He was already late and had received a postcard from his son to say they could not delay it by another day. He demanded his salary and caught his train.

Sarla was sufficiently outraged by his treachery to make the afternoon tea herself, braving the inferno of the kitchen where she seldom had need to venture, and was rewarded by Raja's happy and Ravi's proud beam as she brought out the tea tray to the veranda. But dinner proved something else altogether. Balu showed not the slightest inclination that he meant to help:

he kept to the pantry with grim determination, giving the glasses and silver another polishing rather than take a step into the kitchen. Sarla had a whispered consultation with Ravi, suggesting they take Raja out to India International Centre or the Gymkhana Club for dinner, but Ravi reminded her that the car had gone for servicing and they could go nowhere tonight. Sarla, her sari end tucked in at her waist, wiping the perspiration from her face with her elbow, went back into the kitchen and peered into its recesses to see if the cook had not repented and left some cooked food for them after all, but she found little that she could put together even if she knew how. At one point, she even telephoned Maya to see if her sister would not come to her aid — Maya was known for her superb culinary skill — but there was no answer: Maya and Pravin were out. It was to an embarassingly inadequate repast of sliced cucumber, yoghurt and bread that the three finally sat down — Balu looking as if it were far beneath his dignity to serve such an excuse for a meal, Sarla tight-lipped with anger with herself for failing so blatantly, Ravi trying, with embarrassed sincerity, to thank her for her brave effort, and Raja saying nothing at all, but quietly crumbling the bread beside his plate till he confessed a wish to go to bed early.

But this meant that he was up earlier than ever next morning, and by the time Sarla rose and went wearily kitchenwards to make him tea, he had been awake for hours, performed his yoga and meditation, walked Simba round the garden several times, and was waiting querulously for it. Balu was nowhere to be seen. When Sarla went in search of him — surely he should have been able to make their guest a cup of tea? — she found the door to his room shut, coloured cutouts from film magazines of starlets in swimsuits stuck all over it, and when she called out his name, heard only a groan in reply.

In agitation, she hurried to find Ravi and send him to find out what was wrong. Ravi went in reluctantly, his face bearing an expression of martyrdom, and reappeared to inform her that Balu was suffering from a stomach ache and needed to be taken to a doctor. '*You* do that,' she snapped at him, hardly able to believe this terrible turn in their fortunes.

By lunchtime Raja had made a series of phone calls and discovered that the Dutta-Rays were leaving for Kashmir next day and would be only too delighted to have him accompany them. Sarla stood in the doorway, watching him pack his little bag with beautifully laundered underwear, and wailed, 'But Raja, if you had wanted to go to the hills, we could have gone to Winhaven *ages* ago! I *asked* you, you remember?'

Raja gave her a look that said, 'Winhaven? With you? When I can be on a houseboat in Kashmir with Ila instead?' but of course what he really did was blow her a kiss across the room and whisper conspiratorially, 'Darling, think of the *stories* I'll come back with to entertain you,' and snapped shut the lock on his bag with a satisfied click.

'Simba! Simba!' Ravi put his hands around his mouth and called after the dog who had loped away up to the top of the hill and vanished. Then he turned around to look for Sarla. He could see neither his dog nor his wife – one had gone too far ahead, the other lagged too far behind. He lowered himself onto a rock to catch his breath and picked up a pine cone to toss from hand to hand while he waited, whistling a little tune.

Evening light flooded down from the vast sky, spilling over the pine needles and stones of the hillside. Everything seemed to be bathed in its pale saffron glow. An eagle drifted through the ravine below. He could hear the wind in its feathers, a melancholy whistle.

'Sarla?' he called out finally, and just then saw her come into sight on a turn of the path below him, amongst a mass of blackberry bushes. She seemed to be dragging herself along, her sari trailing in the white dust, her head bowed over the walking stick she held in a slightly trembling hand.

At his voice she looked up and her face was haggard. He stared in surprise: he had not considered this such a difficult climb, or so long a walk. It was where they had always come, to watch the sunset. He himself could still spring up it with no more than a little panting. 'Sarla?' he asked questioningly. 'Want some help, old girl?'

'Coming, coming,' she grumbled, toiling on, 'can't you see I'm coming?'

When she reached the rock where he was waiting, she sank down onto it and wiped her face with the corner of her sari. 'I can't do these climbs any more,' she admitted, with a wince. 'You had better do them alone.'

'Oh, Sarla,' he said, catching up her hand in his, 'I would never want to come up here without you, you know.' They sat there a while, breathing deeply. Beside them a small cricket began to chirp and chirp, and after some time it was no longer light that came spilling down the hill, but shadows.

Winterscape

SHE stands with the baby in her arms in front of the refrigerator, and points at the pictures she has taped on its white enamel surface, each in turn, calling out the names of the people in the photographs. It is a game they play often to pass the time, the great stretches of time they spend alone together. The baby jabs his short pink finger at a photograph, and the mother cries, 'That's Daddy, in his new car!' or 'Susan and cousin Ted, on his first birthday!' and 'Grandma by the Christmas tree!' All these pictures are as bright and festive as bits of tinsel or confetti. Everyone is smiling in them, and there are birthday cakes and Christmas trees, the shining chrome of new cars, bright green lawns and white houses. 'Da-dee!' the baby shouts. 'Soo-sun!' The bright colours make the baby smile. The mother is happy to play the game, and laughs: her baby is learning the names of all the members of the family; he is becoming a part of the family.

Then the baby reaches out and waves an ineffectual hand at

a photograph that is almost entirely white, only a few shades of grey to bring out the shapes and figures in it. There are two, and both are draped in snow-white clothes which cover their shoulders, exposing only the backs of their heads which are white too, and they are standing beside the very same white refrigerator in the same white-painted kitchen, in front of a white-framed window. They are looking out of it, not at the camera but at the snow that is falling past the windowpanes, covering the leafless tree and the wooden fence and the ground outside, providing them with a white snowscape into which they seem nearly to have merged. Nearly.

The baby's pink finger jabs at the white photograph. The mother says nothing immediately: she seems silenced, as if she too has joined the two figures at the window and with them is looking out of the white kitchen into a white world. The photograph somehow calls for silence, creates silence, like snow.

The baby too drops his hand, lowers his head on his mother's shoulder, and yawns. Snow, silence, and sleep: the white picture has filled him with sleep, he is overcome by it. His mother holds him and rocks him, swaying on her feet. She loves the feel of the baby's head on her shoulder; she tucks it under her chin protectively. She swivels around to the window as if she sees the two white figures there now, vanishing into the green dusk of a summer evening. She sings softly into the baby's dark hair: 'Ma and Masi – Ma and Masi together.'

'*Two?*' Beth turned her head on the pillow and stared at him over the top of her glasses, lowering the book she was reading to the rounded dome of her belly under the blue coverlet.

'*Two* tickets? For *whom?*' because she knew Rakesh did not have a father, that his mother was a widow.

'For my mother and my aunt,' he said, in a low, almost sullen voice, sitting on the edge of the bed in his pyjamas and twisting his fingers together. His back was turned to her, his shoulders stooped. Because of the time difference, he had had to place the call to the village in India in the middle of the night.

'Your *aunt?*' Beth heard her own voice escalate. 'Why do we have to pay for your aunt to visit us? Why does *she* have to visit us when the baby is born? I can't have so many guests in the house, Rakesh!'

He turned around towards her slowly, and she saw dark circles under his eyes. Another time they might have caused her to put her finger out to touch those big, bluish pouches, like bruises, but now she felt herself tense at the thought of not just one, but two strangers, foreigners, part of Rakesh's past, invading their house. She had already wished she had not allowed Rakesh to send for his mother to attend to the birth of their child. It had seemed an outlandish, archaic idea even when it was first suggested; now it was positively bizarre. 'Why both of them? We only asked your mother,' she insisted.

Rakesh was normally quick with his smile, his reassuring words, soft and comforting murmurs. He had seemed nervous ever since she became pregnant, more inclined to worry about what she took as a natural process. But she could see it was not that, it was something else that made him brood, silently, on the edge of the bed, the blue pouches hanging under his eyes, and his hands twisted.

'What's the matter?' she said sharply, and took off her glasses and turned over her book. 'What's wrong?'

He roused himself to shake his head, attempted to smile, and failed. Then he lifted up his legs and lay down on the bed, beside her, turning to her with that same brooding expression, not really seeing her. He put out his hand and tried to stroke the hair at her temple. It annoyed her: he was so clearly about to make a request, a difficult request. She tensed, ready to refuse. He ought not to be asking anything of her in her condition. Two guests, two foreigners – at such a time. 'Tell me,' she demanded.

So he began to tell her. 'They are both my mothers, Beth,' he said. 'I have two mothers.'

There were three years between them and those seemed to have made all the difference. Asha was the first child in the family. So delighted was her father that it never crossed his mind she should have been a son. He tossed her up and caught her in his arms and put his face into her neck to make growling sounds that sent her into squeals of laughter. That she was fair-skinned, plump and had curly hair and bright black eyes all pleased him. He liked his wife to dress the child in frilly, flounced, flowered dresses and put ribbons in her hair. She was glad and relieved he was so pleased with his daughter: it could have been otherwise, but he said, 'A pretty daughter is an ornament to the home.'

So Asha grew up knowing she was an ornament, and a joy. She had no hesitation ever in asking for a toy or a sweet, in climbing onto her parents' laps or standing in the centre of a circle to sing or skip.

When Anu was born, three years later, it was different. Although her father bent over her and fondled her head and said nothing to express disappointment, disappointment was in the air. It swaddled baby Anu (no one even remembered her full name, the more majestic Annapurna), and among the first things she heard were the mutterings of the older people in the family who had no compunction about pronouncing their disappointment. And while her mother held her close and defended her against them, baby Anu knew she was in a weak position. So one might have thought, watching her grow. Although she stayed close to her elder sister, clinging to the hem of her dress, shadowing her, and Asha was pleased to have someone so entirely under her control, there remained something hesitant, nervous and tentative about Anu's steps, her movements and speech. Everything about her expressed diffidence.

While Asha proved a natural housekeeper and joined, with gusto, in the cooking, the washing, the sweeping, all those household tasks shared between the women, pinning her chunni back behind her ears, rolling up the sleeves of her kameez, and settling down to kneading the dough, or pounding spices, or rolling out chapatis with a fine vigour, Anu proved sadly incompetent. She managed to get her hand burnt when frying pakoras, took so long to grind chillies that her mother grew impatient and pushed her out of the way, and was too weak to haul up a full bucket of water from the well, needing to do it half a bucket at a time. When visitors filled the house and everything was in an uproar, Anu would try to slip away and make herself invisible and only return when summoned – to be scolded soundly for shirking work. 'Look at your sister,' she was always counselled, and she did, raising her eyes with timid admiration. Asha, used to her sister's ways, gave her a wink and slipped her one of the snacks or sweets she had missed. An understanding grew between them, strengthened by strand upon strand upon strand of complicity.

Later, sons were born to their parents, and the pressure, the tension in their relationships with their daughters was relieved. Good-naturedly, the father allowed both of them to go to school. 'What is the harm?' he asked the elderly critics of this unusual move. 'These days it is good for girls to be educated. One day, who knows, they may work in an office – or a bank!'

That certainly did not happen. Another generation would be born and raised before any girl in that Punjab village became an office clerk or a bank teller. Asha and Anu had a few years in the local government school where they wore blue cotton kameezes with white chunnis, and white gym shoes, and sat on benches learning the Punjabi alphabet and their numbers. Here the scales may well have tipped the other way, because Asha found the work ferociously difficult and grew hot and bothered as she tried to work out problems in addition and subtraction or to read her lessons from the tattered, illustrated text books, while Anu discovered an unexpected nimbleness of mind that skipped about the numbers with the agility of a young goat, and scampered through the letters quite friskily. Asha threw her sister exasperated looks but did not mind so much when Anu took over her homework and did it for her in her beautiful hand. Anu drew praise when she wrote essays on 'The Cow' and 'My Favourite Festival' – but, alas, the latter proved to be her swan song because at this point Asha turned fifteen and the family found her a bridegroom and married her off and Anu had to stay home from then on to help her mother.

Asha's bridegroom was a large man, not so young, but it did not matter because he owned so much land and cattle. He had a great handlebar moustache and a turban and Anu was terrified for Asha when she first saw him, but was later to find no cause for terror: he was a kindly, good-natured man who clearly adored his bright-eyed, quick-tongued, lively young wife and was generous to her and to her entire family. His voice was unexpectedly soft and melodious, and he often regaled his visitors, or a gathering in the village, with his songs. Asha — who had plenty of talents but not artistic ones — looked at him with admiration then, sitting back on her haunches and cupping her chin in her hands which were bedecked with the rings and bracelets he had given her.

They often asked Anu to come and stay with them. Asha found she was so accustomed to having her younger sister at her heels, she really could not do without her. She might have done, had she had children, but, though many were born to her, they were either stillborn or died soon after birth, none living for more than a few days. This created an emptiness in the big house so full of goods and comforts, and Asha grew querulous and plaintive, a kind of bitterness informing her every gesture and expression, while her husband became prone to depression which no one would have predicted earlier. Anu often came upon him seated in an armchair at the end of the veranda, or up on the flat roof of the house in the cool evenings, looking out with an expression of deep melancholy across his fields to the horizon where the white spire and the golden dome of the Sikh temple stood against the sky. He left the work on the farm to a trusted headman to supervise and became idle himself, exasperating Asha who tended to throw herself into every possible activity with determined vigour and thought a man should too.

After yet another miscarriage, Asha roused herself with a grim wilfulness to join in the preparation for Anu's wedding, arranged by the parents to a clerk in a neighbouring town, a sullen, silent young man with large teeth and large hands that he rubbed together all the time. Anu kept her face and her tears hidden throughout the wedding, as brides did, and Asha was both consoling and encouraging, as women were.

Unexpectedly, that unpromising young man who blinked through his spectacles and could scarcely croak one sentence at a time, showed no hesitation whatsoever when it came to fathering a child. Nor did Anu, who was so slight of frame and mousy in manner, seem to be in any way handicapped as a woman or mother – her child was born easily, and it was a son. A round, black-haired, red-cheeked boy who roared lustily for his milk and thrashed out with his legs and grabbed with his hands, clearly meant for survival and success.

If Anu and her husband were astonished by him, it could scarcely have matched Asha and her husband's wonder. They were enthralled by the boy: he was the child of their dreams, their thwarted hopes and desires. Anu lay back and watched how Asha scooped Rakesh up into her large, soft arms, how she cradled and kissed him, then how her husband took him from her, wrapped in the candy pink wool shawl knitted by Asha, and crooned over him. She was touched and grateful for Asha's competence, as adept at handling the baby as in churning butter or making sweets. Anu stayed in bed, letting her sister fuss over both her and the baby – making Anu special milk and almond and jaggery drinks in tall metal tumblers, keeping the baby happy and content, massaging him with mustard oil, feeding him sips of sweetened milk from a silver shell, tickling him till he smiled.

Anu's husband looked on, awkwardly, too nervous to hold his own child: small creatures made him afraid; he never failed to kick a puppy or a kitten out of his way, fiercely. Anu rose from her bed occasionally to make a few tentative gestures of motherhood but soon relinquished them, one by one, first letting Asha feed the baby and dress him, then giving up attempts to nurse the boy and letting Asha take over the feeding.

At the first hint of illness – actually, the baby was teething which caused a tummy upset – Asha bundled him up in his blanket and took him home, promising, 'I'll bring him back as soon as he is well. Now you go and rest, Anu, you haven't slept and you look sick yourself.'

When Anu went to fetch him after a week, she came upon Asha's husband, sitting on that upright chair of his on the veranda, but now transformed. He had the baby on his knee and was hopping him up and down while singing a rhyme, and his eyes sparkled as vivaciously as the child's. Instead of taking her son from him, Anu held back, enjoying the scene. Noticing her at last, the large man in the turban beamed at her. 'A prince!' he said, 'and one day he will have all my fields, my cattle, the dairy, the cane-crushing factory, everything. He will grow up to be a prince!'

Rakesh's first birthday was to be celebrated at Asha's house – 'We will do it in style,' she said, revealing how little she thought Anu and her husband were capable of achieving it. Preparations went on for weeks beforehand. There was to be a feast for the whole village. A goat was to be slaughtered and roasted, and the women in the family were busy making sweets and delicacies with no expense spared: Asha's husband was seeing to that. He himself went out to shoot partridges for the festive dinner, setting out before dawn into the rippling grainfields and calling back to the women to have the fire ready for his return.

Those were his last words – to have the fire ready. 'As if he knew', wept Asha's mother, 'that it was the funeral pyre we would light.' Apparently there had been an accident with the gun. It had gone off unexpectedly and the bullet had pierced his shoulder and a lung: he had bled to death. There were no birthday festivities for one-year-old Rakesh.

Knowing that the one thing that could comfort Asha was the presence of the baby in her arms, Anu refrained from suggesting she take him home. At first she had planned to leave the boy with her widowed sister for the first month of mourning, then drew it out to two and even three months. When her husband, taunted by his own family for his failure to establish himself as head of his household, ordered her to bring their son home, Anu surprised herself by answering, 'Let him be. Asha needs him. We can have more sons for ourselves.' Their house was empty and melancholy – it had always been a mean place, a narrow set of rooms in the bazaar, with no sunlight or air – but she sat in its gloom, stitching clothes for her rapidly growing son, a chunni drawn over her head, a picture of acceptance that her husband was not able to disturb, except briefly, with fits of violence.

After one of these, they would go and visit the boy, with gifts, and Rakesh came to look upon his parents as a visiting aunt and uncle, who offered him sweets and toys with a dumbly appeasing, appealing air. No one remembered when he started calling them Masi and Masa. Asha he already addressed as Ma: it was so clearly her role.

Anu had been confident other children would follow. She hoped for a daughter next time, somehow feeling a daughter might be more like her, and more likely to stay with her. But Rakesh had his second and third birthday in Asha's house, and there was no other child. Anu's husband looked discouraged now, and resentful, his own family turning into a chorus of mocking voices. He stayed away at work for long hours; there were rumours – quickly brought to Anu's attention – that he had taken to gambling, and drugs, and some even hinted at having seen him in quarters of the town where respectable people did not go. She was not too perturbed: their relationship was a furtive, nocturnal thing that never survived daylight. She was concerned, of course, when he began to look ill, to break out in boils and rashes, and come down with frequent fevers, and she nursed him in her usual bungling, tentative way. His family came to take over, criticising her sharply for her failings as a nurse, but he only seemed to grow worse, and died shortly before Rakesh's fifth birthday. His family set up a loud lament and clearly blamed her for the way he had dwindled away in spite of their care. She packed her belongings – in the same tin trunk in which she had brought them as a bride, having added nothing more to them – and went to live with Asha – and the child.

In the dark, Beth found it was she who was stroking the hair at Rakesh's temple now, and he who lay stretched out with his hands folded on his chest and his eyes staring at the ceiling.

'Then the woman you call Ma – she is really your aunt?' Beth queried.

Rakesh gave a long sigh. 'I always knew her as my mother.'

'And your aunt is your real mother? When did they tell you?'

'I don't know,' he admitted. 'I grew up knowing it – perhaps people spoke of it in the village, but when you are small you don't question. You just accept.'

'But didn't your *real* mother ever tell you, or try to take you away?'

'No!' he exclaimed. 'That's just it, Beth. She never did – she had given me to her sister, out of love, out of sympathy when her husband died. She never tried to break up the relationship I had with her. It was out of love.' He tried to explain again, 'The love sisters feel.'

Beth, unlike Rakesh, had a sister. Susan. She thought of her now, living with her jobless, worthless husband in a trailer somewhere in Manitoba with a string of children. The thought of handing over her child to her was so bizarre that it made her snort. 'I know I couldn't give my baby to Susan for anything,' she declared, removing her hand from his temple and placing it on her belly.

'You don't know, you can't say — what may happen, what things one may do —'

'*Of course* I know,' she said, more loudly. 'Nothing, no one, could make me do that. Give my baby away?' Her voice became shrill and he turned on his side, closing his eyes to show her he did not wish to continue the conversation.

She understood that gesture but she persisted. 'But didn't they ever fight? Or disagree about the way you were brought up? Didn't they have different ideas of how to do that? You know, I've told Susan —'

He sighed again. 'It was not like that. They understood each other. Ma looked after me — she cooked for me and fed me, made me sit down on a mat and sat in front of me and fed me with her own hands. And what a cook she is! Beth, you'll love —' he broke off, knowing he was going too far, growing foolish now. 'And Masi,' he recovered himself, 'she took me by the hand to school. In the evening, she lit the lamp and made me show her my books. She helped me with my lessons — and I think learned with me. She is a reader, Beth, like you,' he was able to say with greater confidence.

'But weren't they jealous of each other — of one for cooking for you and feeding you, and the other for sharing your lessons? Each was doing what the other didn't, after all.'

He caught her hand, on the coverlet, to stop her talking. 'It wasn't like that,' he said again, and wished she would be silent so he could remember for himself that brick-walled courtyard in the village, the pump gushing out the sweet water from the tube well, the sounds of cattle stirring in the sheaves of fodder in the sheds, the can of frothing milk the dairyman brought to the door, the low earthen stove over which his mother – his aunt – stirred a pan in the smoky dimness of dawn, making him tea. The pigeons in the rafters, cooing, a feather drifting down –

'Well, I suppose I'll be seeing them both, then – and I'll find out for myself,' Beth said, a bit grimly, and snapped off the light.

'Never heard of anything so daft,' pronounced her mother, pouring out a cup of coffee for Beth who sat at her kitchen table with her elbows on its plastic cover and her chin cupped in her hands. Doris was still in her housecoat and slippers, going about her morning in the sunlit kitchen. Beth had come early.

When Beth did not reply, Doris planted her hands on the table and stared into her brooding face. 'Well, isn't it?' she demanded. 'Whoever heard of such a thing? Rakesh having two mothers! Why ever didn't he tell us before?'

'He told me about them both of course,' Beth flared up, and began to stir her coffee. 'He talked of them as his mother and aunt. I knew they were both widows, lived together, that's all.'

Doris looked as if she had plenty more to say on the subject than that. She tightened the belt around her red-striped housecoat and sat down squarely across from Beth. 'Looks as if he never told you who his mother was though, or his father. The real ones, I mean. I call that peculiar, Beth, pec-u-liar!'

Beth stirred resentfully. 'I s'pose he hardly thinks of it that way – he was a baby when it happened. He says he grew up just accepting it. They *love* each other, he said.'

Doris scratched at her head with one hand, rattled the coffee cup in its saucer with the other. 'Two sisters loving each other – that much? That's what's so daft – who in her right mind would give away her baby to her sister just like that? I mean, would you hand yours over to Susan? And would Susan take it? I mean, as if it were a birthday present!'

'Oh, Mum!'

'Now you've spilt your coffee! Wait, I'll get a sponge. Don't get up. You're getting big, girl. You OK? You mustn't mind me.'

'I'm OK, Mum, but now I'm going to have *two* women visiting. Rakesh's mum would be one thing, but two of 'em together – I don't know.'

'That's what I say,' Doris added quickly. 'And all that expense – why's he sending them tickets? I thought they had money: he keeps talking about that farm as if they were landlords –'

'Oh, that's where he grew up, Mum. They sold it long ago – that's what paid for his education at McGill, you know. That *costs*.'

'What – it cost them the whole farm? He's always talking about how big it was –'

'They sold it a bit at a time. They helped pay for our house, too, and then set up his practice.'

'Hmm,' said Doris, as she shook a cigarette out of a packet and put it in her mouth.

'Oh, Mum, I can't stand smoke now! It makes me nauseous – you know that –' Beth protested.

'Sorry, love,' Doris said, and laid down the matchbox she had picked up but with the cigarette still between her lips. 'I'm just worried about you – dealing with two Indian women – in your condition –'

'I guess they know about babies,' Beth said hopefully.

'But do they know about Canada?' Doris came back smartly, as one who had learned. 'And about the Canadian *winter?*'

They thought they did – from Rakesh's dutiful, although not very informative, letters over the years. After Rakesh had graduated from the local college, it was Asha who insisted he go abroad 'for further studies'. Anu would not have had the courage to suggest it, and had no money of her own to spend, but here was another instance of her sister's courage and boldness. Asha had seen all the bright young people of the village leave and told Anu, 'He' – meaning her late husband – 'wanted Rakesh to study abroad. "We will give him the best education," he had said, so I am only doing what he told me to.' She tucked her widow's white chunni behind her ears and lifted her chin, looking proud. When Anu raised the matter of expense, she waved her hand – so competent at raising the boy, at running the farm, and now at handling the accounts. 'We will sell some of the land. Where is the need for so much? Rakesh will never be a farmer,' she said. So Rakesh began to apply to foreign universities, and although his two mothers felt tightness in their chests at the prospect of his leaving them, they also swelled with pride to think he might do so, the first in the family to leave the country 'for further studies'. When he had completed his studies – the two women selling off bits and pieces of the land to pay for them till there was nothing left but the old farmhouse – he wrote to tell them he had been offered jobs by several firms. They wiped their eyes with the corners of their chunnis, weeping for joy at his success and the sorrowful knowledge that he would not come back. Instead, they received letters about his achievements: his salary, his promotion, and with it the apartment in the city, then his own office and practice, photographs accompanying each as proof.

Then, one day, the photograph that left them speechless: it showed him standing with his arm around a girl, a blonde girl, at an office party. She was smiling. She had fair hair cut short and wore a green hairband and a green dress. Rakesh was beaming. He had grown rather fat, his stomach bulging out of a striped shirt, above a leather belt with a big buckle. He was also rather bald. The girl looked small and slim and young beside him. Rakesh did not tell them how old she was, what family she came from, what schooling she had had, when was the wedding, should they come, and other such particulars of importance to them. Rakesh, when he wrote, managed to avoid almost all such particulars, mentioning only that the wedding would be small, merely an official matter of registration at the town hall, they need not trouble to come – as they had ventured to suggest.

They were hurt. They tried to hide it from their neighbours as they went around with boxes of tinsel-spread sweets as gifts to celebrate the far-off occasion. So when the letter arrived announcing Beth's punctual pregnancy and the impending birth, they did not again make the mistake of tactful enquiries: Anu's letter stated with unaccustomed boldness their intention to travel to Canada and see their grandchild for themselves. That was her term – 'our grandchild'.

Yet it was with the greatest trepidation that they set out on this adventure. Everyone in the village was encouraging and supportive. Many of them had flown to the US, to Canada, to England, to visit their children abroad. It had become almost commonplace for the families to travel to New Delhi, catch a plane and fly off to some distant continent, bearing bundles and boxes full of the favourite pickles, chutneys and sweets of their far-flung progeny. Stories abounded of these goodies being confiscated on arrival at the airports, taken away by indignant customs officers to be burnt: 'He asked me, "What is *this*? What is *this*?" He had never seen mango pickle before, can you believe?' 'He didn't know what is betel nut! "Beetle? You are bringing in an insect?" he asked!' – and of being stranded at airports by great blizzards or lightning strikes by airline staff – 'We were lucky we had taken our bedroll and could spread out on the floor and sleep' – and of course they vied with each other with reports of their sons' and daughters' palatial mansions, immense cars, stocked refrigerators, prodigies of shopping in the most extensive of department stores. They brought back with them electrical appliances, cosmetics, watches, these symbols of what was 'foreign'.

The two mothers had taken no part in this, saying, 'We can get those here too,' and contenting themselves by passing around the latest photographs of Rakesh and his wife and their home in Toronto. Now that they too were to join this great adventure, they became nervous – even Asha did. Young, travelled daughters and granddaughters of old friends came around to reassure them: 'Auntie, it is not difficult at all! Just buy a ticket at the booth, put it in the slot, and step into the subway. It will take you where you like,' or 'Over there you won't need kerosene or coal for the stove, Auntie. You have only to switch on the stove, it will light by itself,' or 'You won't need to wash your clothes, Auntie. They have machines, you put everything in, with soap, it washes by itself.' The two women wondered if these self-confident youngsters were pulling their legs: they were not reassured.

Every piece of information, meant to help, threw them into greater agitation. They were convinced they would be swallowed up by the subway if they went out, or electrocuted at home if they stayed in. By the time the day of their departure came around, they were feverish with anxiety and sleeplessness. Anu would gladly have abandoned the plan – but Asha reminded her that Rakesh had sent them tickets, his first present to them after leaving home, how could they refuse?

It was ten years since Rakesh had seen his mothers, and he had forgotten how thinly they tended to dress, how unequipped they might be. Beth's first impression of them as they came out of the immigration control area, wheeling a trolley between them with their luggage precariously balanced on it, was of their wisps of widows' white clothing – muslin, clearly – and slippers flapping at their feet. Rakesh was embarrassed by their skimpy apparel, Beth unexpectedly moved. She had always thought of them as having so much; now her reaction was: they have so little!

She took them to the stores at once to fit them out with overcoats, gloves, mufflers – and woollen socks. They drew the line at shoes: they had never worn shoes, could not fit their feet into them, insisting on wearing their sandals with thick socks instead. She brought them back barely able to totter out of the car and up the drive, weighed down as they were by great duffle coats that kept their arms lifted from their sides, with their hands fitted into huge gloves, and with their heads almost invisible under the wrappings of woollen mufflers. Under it all, their white cotton kameezes hung out like rags of their past, sadly.

When Doris came around to visit them, she brought along

all the spare blankets she had in her apartment, presciently. 'Thought you'd be cold,' she told them. 'I went through the war in England, and I know what that's like, I can tell you. And it isn't half cold yet. Wait till it starts to snow.' They smiled eagerly, in polite anticipation.

While Beth and Doris bustled about, 'settling them in', Rakesh stood around, unexpectedly awkward and ill at ease. After the first ecstatic embrace and the deep breath of their lingering odour of the barnyard and woodsmoke and the old soft muslin of their clothing, their sparse hair, he felt himself in their way and didn't know quite what to do with himself or with them. It was Beth who made them tea and tested their English while Rakesh sat with his feet apart, cracking his knuckles and smiling somewhat vacantly.

At the table, it was different: his mothers unpacked all the foods they had brought along, tied up in small bundles or packed in small boxes, and coaxed him to eat, laughing as they remembered how he had pestered them for these as a child. To them, he was still that: a child, and now he ate, and a glistening look of remembrance covered his face like a film of oil on his fingers, but he also glanced sideways at Beth, guiltily, afraid of betraying any disloyalty to her. She wrinkled her nose slightly, put her hand on her belly and excused herself from eating on account of her pregnancy. They nodded sympathetically and promised to make special preparations for her.

On weekends, Beth insisted he take them out and show them the sights, and they dutifully allowed themselves to be led into his car, and then around museums, up radio towers and into department stores — but they tended to become carsick on these excursions, foot-weary in museums and confused in stores. They clearly preferred to stay in. That was painful, and the only way out of the boredom was to bring home videos and put them on. Then everyone could put their heads back and sleep, or pretend to sleep.

On weekdays, in desperation, Beth too took to switching on the television set, tuned to programmes she surmised were blandly innocent, and imagined they would sit together on the sofa and find amusement in the nature, travel and cooking programmes. Unfortunately these had a way of changing when her back was turned and she would return to find them in a state of shock from watching a torrid sex scene or violent battle taking place before their affronted and disbelieving eyes. They sat side by side with their feet dangling and their eyes screwed up, munching on their dentures with fear at the popping of guns, the exploding of bombs and grunting of naked bodies. Their relief when she suggested a break for tea was palpable. Once in the kitchen, the kettle whistling shrilly, cups standing ready with the threads of tea bags dangling out of them, they seemed reluctant to leave the sanctuary. The kitchen was their great joy, once they had got used to the shiny enamel and chrome and up-to-date gadgetry. They became expert at punching the buttons of the microwave although they never learned what items could and what could not be placed in it. To Rakesh's surprise it was Anu who seemed to comprehend the rules better, she who peered at any scrap of writing, trying to decipher some meaning. Together the two would open the refrigerator twenty times in one morning, never able to resist looking in at its crowded, illuminated shelves; that reassurance of food seemed to satisfy them on some deep level – their eyes gleamed and they closed the door on it gently, with a dreamy expression.

Still, the resources of the kitchen were not limitless. Beth found they had soon run through them, and the hours dragged for her, in the company of the two mothers. There were just so many times she could ask Doris to come over and relieve her, and just so many times she could invent errands that would allow them all to escape from the house so crowded with their hopes, expectations, confusion and disappointments. She knew Rakesh disappointed them. She watched them trying to re-create what he had always described to her as his most warmly close and intimate relationship, and invariably failing. The only way they knew to do this was to cook him the foods of his childhood – as best they could reproduce these in this strange land – or retail the gossip of the village, not realising he had forgotten the people they spoke of, had not the slightest interest in who had married whom, or sold land or bought cattle. He would give embarassed laughs, glance at Beth in appeal, and find reasons to stay late at work. She was exasperated by his failure but also secretly relieved to see how completely he had transformed himself into a husband, a Canadian, and, guiltily, she too dragged out her increasingly frequent escapes – spending the afternoon at her mother's house, describing to a fascinated Doris the village ways of these foreign mothers, or meeting girlfriends for coffee, going to the library to read child-rearing manuals – then returning in a rush of concern for the two imprisoned women at home.

She had spent one afternoon at the library, deep in an old stuffed chair in an undisturbed corner she knew, reading – something she found she could not do at home where the two mothers would watch her as she read, intently, as if waiting to see where it would take her and when she would be done – when she became aware of the light fading, darkness filling the tall window under which she sat. When she looked up, she was startled to see flakes of snow drifting through the dark, minute as tiny bees flying in excited hordes. They flew faster and faster as she watched, and in no time they would grow larger, she knew. She closed the magazine hastily, replaced it on the rack, put on her beret and gloves, picked up her bag and went out to the car outside. She opened the door and got in clumsily; she was so large now it was difficult to fit behind the steering wheel.

The streets were very full, everyone hurrying home before the snowfall became heavier. Her windscreen wiper going furiously, Beth drove home carefully. The first snowfall generally had its element of surprise; something childish in her responded with excitement. But this time she could only think of how surprised the two mothers would be, how much more intense their confinement.

When she let herself into the house with her key, she could look straight down the hall to the kitchen, and there she saw them standing, at the window, looking out to see the snow collect on the twigs and branches of the bare cherry tree and the tiles of the garden shed and the top of the wooden fence outside. Their white cotton saris were wrapped about them like shawls, their two heads leaned against each other as they peered out, speechlessly.

They did not hear her, they were so absorbed in the falling of the snow and the whitening of the stark scene on the other side of the glass pane. She shut the door silently, slipped into her bedroom and fetched the camera from where it lay on the closet shelf. Then she came out into the hall again and, standing there, took a photograph.

Later, when it was developed – together with the first pictures of the baby – she showed the mothers the print, and they put their hands to their mouths in astonishment. 'Why didn't you tell us?' they said. 'We didn't know – our backs were turned.' Beth wanted to to tell them it didn't matter, it was their postures that expressed everything, but then they would have wanted to know what 'everything' was, and she found she did not want to explain, she did not want words to break the silent completeness of that small, still scene. It was as complete, and as fragile, after all, as a snow crystal.

The birth of the baby broke through it, of course. The sisters revived as if he were a reincarnation of Rakesh. They wanted to hold him, flat on the palms of their hands, or sit crosslegged on the sofa and rock him by pumping one knee up and down, and could not at all understand why Beth insisted they place him in his cot in a darkened bedroom instead. 'He has to learn to go to sleep by himself,' she told them when he cried and cried in protest and she refused to give them permission to snatch him up to their flat bosoms and console him.

They could not understand the rituals of baby care that Beth imposed – the regular feeding and sleeping times, the boiling and sterilising of bottles and teats, the cans of formula and the use of disposable diapers. The first euphoria and excitement soon led to little nervous dissensions and explosions, then to dejection. Beth was too absorbed in her child to care.

The winter proved too hard, too long for the visitors. They began to fall ill, to grow listless, to show signs of depression and restlessness. Rakesh either did not notice or pretended not to, so that when Beth spoke of it one night in their bedroom, he asked if she were not 'over-reacting', one of his favourite terms. 'Ask them, just ask them,' she retorted. 'How can I?' he replied. 'Can I say to them "D'you want to go home?" They'll think I want them to.' She flung her arms over her head in exasperation. 'Why can't you just talk to each other?' she asked.

She was restless too, eager to bring to an end a visit that had gone on too long. The two little old women were in her way, underfoot, as she hurried between cot and kitchen. She tried to throw them sympathetic smiles but knew they were more like grimaces. She often thought about the inexplicable relationship of these two women, how Masi, small, mousy Masi, had borne Rakesh and then given him over to Ma, her sister. What could have made her do that? How could she have? Thinking of her own baby, the way he filled her arms and fitted against her breast, Beth could not help but direct a piercing, perplexed stare at them. She knew she would not give up her baby for anything, anyone, certainly not to her sister Susan who was hardly capable of bringing up her own, and yet these two had lived their lives ruled by that one impulse, totally unnatural to her. They looked back at her, questioningly, sensing her hostility.

And eventually they asked Rakesh — very hesitantly, delicately, but clearly after having discussed the matter between themselves and having come to a joint decision. They wanted to go home. The baby had arrived safely, and Beth was on her feet again, very much so. And it was too much for her, they said, a strain. No, no, she had not said a thing, of course not, nothing like that, and nor had he, even inadvertently. They were happy — they had been happy — but now — and they coughed and coughed, in embarrassment as much as on account of the cold. And out of pity he cut short their fumbling explanations, and agreed to book their seats on a flight home. Yes, he and Beth would come and visit them, with the baby, as soon as he was old enough to travel.

This was the right thing to say. Their creased faces lifted up to him in gratitude. He might have spilt some water on wilting plants: they revived; they smiled; they began to shop for presents for everyone at home. They began to think of those at home, laugh in anticipation of seeing home again.

At the farewell in the airport – he took them there while Beth stayed at home with the baby, who had a cold – they cast their tender, grateful looks upon him again, then turned to wheel their trolley with its boxes and trunks away, full of gifts for family and neighbours. He watched as their shoulders, swathed in their white chunnis, and their bent white heads, turned away from him and disappeared. He lifted a fist to his eyes in an automatic gesture, then sighed with relief and headed for his car waiting in the grey snow.

At home Beth had put the baby to sleep in his cot. She had cooked dinner, and on hearing Rakesh enter, she lit candles on the table, as though it were a celebration. He looked at her questioningly but she only smiled. She had cooked his favourite pasta. He sat at the table and lifted his fork, trying to eat. Why, what was she celebrating? He found a small, annoying knot of resentment fastened onto the fork at her evident pleasure at being alone with him and her baby again. He kept the fork suspended to look at her, to demand if this were so, and then saw, over her shoulder, the refrigerator with its array of the photographs and memos she liked to tape to its white enamel surface. What caught his eye was the photograph she had newly taped to it – with the view of the white window, and the two widows in white, and the whirling snow.

He put down his forkful of pasta. 'Rakesh? Rakesh?' Beth

asked a few times, then turned to look herself. Together they stared at the winterscape.

'Why?' he asked.

Beth shrugged. 'Let it be,' she said.

Diamond Dust
A Tragedy

'THAT dog will kill me, kill me one day!' Mrs Das moaned, her hand pressed to her large, soft, deep bosom when Diamond leapt at the chop she had cooked and set on the table for Mr Das; or when Diamond dashed past her, bumping against her knees and making her collapse against the door when she was going to receive a parcel from the postman who stood there, shaking, as he fended off the black lightning hurled at him. 'Diamond! Why did you call him Diamond? He is Satan, a shaitan, a devil. Call him Devil instead,' Mrs Das cried as she washed and bandaged the ankle of a grandchild who had only run after a ball and had that shaitan snap his teeth over his small foot.

But to Mr Das he was Diamond, and had been Diamond ever since he had bought him, as a puppy of an indecipherable breed, blunt-faced, with his wet nose gleaming and paws flailing for action. Mr Das could not explain how he had come upon that name. Feebly, he would laugh when questioned by friends he met in the park at five o'clock in the morning when he took Diamond for a walk before leaving for the office, and say, 'Yes, yes, black diamond, you see, black diamond.' But when C. P. Biswas, baring his terribly stained yellow teeth in an unpleasant laugh, said, 'Ah, coal – then call him that, my dear fellow, coal, koyla – and we would all understand.'

Never. Never would Mr Das do such a thing to his Diamond. If his family and friends only knew what names he thought up for the puppy, for the dog, in secret, in private – he did not exactly blush but he did laugh to himself, a little sheepishly. And yet his eyes shone when he saw how Diamond's coat gleamed as he streaked across the park after a chipmunk, or when he greeted the dog on his return from work before greeting Mrs Das, his grandchildren, or anyone at all, with the joyful cry, 'Diamond, my friend!'

Mrs Das had had a premonition – had she not known Mr Das since she had been a fourteen-year-old bride, he a nineteen-year-old bridegroom? – when she saw him bring that puppy home, cuddling it in his old brown jumper, lowering his voice to a whisper and his step to a tiptoe, as if afraid of alarming the sleeping creature. 'Get some warm milk – don't heat it too much – just warm it a little – and get some cotton wool.' She had stared at him. 'Not even about our own children, not even your first-born son, or your grandchildren, have you made so much of as of that dog,' she had told him then.

She repeated it, not once, or twice, or thrice, but at regular intervals throughout that shining stretch of Mr Das's life when Diamond evolved from a round, glossy cocoon into a trembling, faltering fat puppy that bent its weak legs and left puddles all over Mrs Das's clean, fresh floors, and then into an awkwardly – so lovably awkwardly – lumbering young dog

that Mr Das led around on a leash across the dusty maidan of
Bharti Nagar, delighting in the children who came up to
admire the creature but politely fearful of those who begged,
'Uncle, let me hold him! Let me take him for a walk, Uncle!'
Only in the Lodi Gardens did he dare slip Diamond off his
leash for the joy of seeing him race across that lawn after
chipmunks that scurried up trees, furiously chattering and
whisking their tails in indignation while Diamond sat at the
foot of the tree, whining, his eyes lustrous with desire.
'Diamond, Diamond,' Mr Das would call, and lumbering up
to him, would fondle his head, his ears and murmur words of
love to entice him away from the scolding creatures in the
leaves.

But there were times when Mr Das went beyond that, times
that his friends and colleagues whom he met daily on their
morning walks were astounded, if not scandalised, to witness,
so much so that they could hardly speak of it to each other. Mr
Das had so clearly taken leave of his senses, and it made them
worry: how could a reputable government servant, a colleague, fall so low? They had caught him, as portly and stiff as
any of them, romping ridiculously in a rose garden enclosed
by crumbling, half-ruined walls that he had imagined hid him
from view, chasing or letting himself be chased around the
rose beds by a wild-with-excitement dog whose barks rent the
peace of the morning park. They hardly knew how to tell him
he was making a fool of himself. Instead, settling down on a
bench in the shade of a neem tree and with a view of the Lodi
tombs, watching parrots emerge from the alcoves and shoot up
into the brilliant summer air, they discussed it between
themselves gravely, and with distaste, as became their age and
station – the decent, elderly civil servants with a life of service
and sobriety behind them.

'There was that time Raman Kutty's grandchild was visiting him from Madras, and he would bring her to the park. He would even push the pram, like an ayah. During that visit, he couldn't speak of anything, or say anything but "Look, she has a new tooth," or "See her sucking her toe, so sweet." And that child, with its crossed eyes –'

'Tch, tch,' another reproved him for his ill-mannered outburst.

But the outburst was really occasioned by Mr Das, and the sight they had all had of him kicking up his heels like a frolicking goat in the rose garden, oblivious of the gardeners who sat on their haunches in the shade, smoking and keeping a vigilant eye on their rose beds.

'Look, here he comes with that wretched beast,' C. P. Biswas cried out. He was never in very good humour in the mornings; they all knew it had to do with his digestive system and its discomforts: they had often come upon him seated in the waiting room of the homeopath's clinic which was open to the marketplace and in full view of those who shopped there for their eggs and vegetables. 'I think he should be told. What do you say, should we tell him?'

'Tell him what, C. P.?' asked the mild-mannered A. P. Bose.

'That such behaviour is not at all becoming!' exclaimed C. P. Biswas. 'After all, a civil servant – serving in the Department of Mines and Minerals – what will people say?'

'Who?'

'Who? Look, there is the Under Secretary walking over there with his wife. What if he sees? Or the retired Joint Secretary who is doing his yoga exercises over there by the tank. You think they don't know him? He has to be told – we are here to remind him.'

Unfortunately Mr Das chose not to join them that morning.

He walked smartly past them, hanging onto Diamond's leash and allowing Diamond to drag him forward at a pace more suited to a youth of twenty, and an athletic one at that. He merely waved at his friends, seeing them arranged in a row on the bench, and, clearly not intending to join their sedate company, disappeared behind a magnificent grove of bamboos that twittered madly with mynah birds.

C. P. Biswas was beginning to rumble and threaten to explode but A. P. Bose drew out the morning newspaper from his briefcase, unclasped the pen from his pocket, and tactfully asked for help in completing the day's crossword puzzle.

Of course their disapproval was as nothing compared to that of Mrs Das who did not merely observe Mr Das's passion from a distance but was obliged to live with it. It was she who had to mop up the puddles from her gleaming floors when Diamond was a puppy, she who had to put up with the reek of dog in a home that had so far been aired and cleaned and sunned and swept and dusted till one could actually see the walls and floors thinning from the treatment to which they had been subjected. Her groans and exclamations as she swept up (or, rather, had the little servant girl sweep up) tufts of dog's hair from her rugs – and sometimes even her sofas and armchairs – were loud and rang with lament. Of course she refused to go to the butcher's shop for buffalo meat for the dog – she would not go near that stinking hellhole on the outskirts of the marketplace, and Mr Das had to brave its bloody, reeking, fly-coated territory himself, clutching a striped plastic bag close to him with one hand and pressing a thickly folded handkerchief to his nose with the other – but, still, she had to sacrifice one of her cooking pots to it, and tolerate the bubbling and frothing of the meat stew on the back burner of her stove. During the hour that it took, she would retreat to the veranda and sit there in a wicker chair, fanning herself with melodramatic flair.

'But do you want the dog to starve? Do you think a dog such as Diamond can be brought up on bread and milk?' Mr Das pleaded. 'How would he grow? How would he live?'

'Why not? I have heard even of tigers being fed on milk. It is true. Absolutely. Don't give me those looks, D. P. There was a yogi in Jubbulpore when I was a girl, he lived in a cave outside the city, with a pet tiger, and it was said he fed it only on milk. He brought it to town on festival days, I saw it with my own eyes. It was healthy, that milk-fed tiger, and as harmless as a kitten.'

'But I am not a yogi and Diamond is not a yogi's pet. What about that cat you had? Did it not kill sparrows and eat fish?'

'*My* cat was the cleanest creature this earth has ever known!' Mrs Das cried, holding the fan to her breast for a moment, in tribute to the deceased pet. 'Yes, she enjoyed a little fish from my plate – but she ate so neatly, so cleanly –'

'But fish, wasn't it? And sparrows? You see, an animal's nature cannot be changed simply because it is domesticated, Sheila. That tiger you speak of, it is quite possible that one day it turned upon the yogi and made a meal of him –'

'What are you saying?' Mrs Das cried, and began to flutter her fan again. 'That yogi lived to be a hundred years old!' And Mr Das went off, muttering disbelievingly, to dish out the meat stew for Diamond in an earthenware bowl in the courtyard and then carefully shut the kitchen door behind him so Diamond could not drag one of the bones into the house to chew on a rug as he very much liked to do and would do if not prevented.

The children of the neighbourhood were more appreciative, and properly admiring, than his wife, Mr Das felt as he walked Diamond past the small stucco villas set in their gardens of mango trees and oleander hedges, attracting flocks of them as he went. But he was not so besotted or blinded as to ignore the need always to have Diamond firmly secured on his leash when children were around. He was not unaware that once he had turned his back, or if they had come upon Diamond when he was not around, they were quite capable of arousing the dog to a frenzy by teasing him. 'We were only playing, Uncle!' they would cry reproachfully after Diamond had broken loose and chased them until they fell sprawling in the dust, or even nipped at their heels as they ran. 'That is *not* how to play with a dog,' he reproved them severely. 'You must *not* wave a stick at him. You must *not* pick up a stone. You must *not* run –'

'If we don't run, he'll bite, Uncle! See, he bit Ranu on her heel –'

'Nonsense,' he retorted, 'that's only a scratch,' and Mr Das walked quickly away, Diamond held closely, protectively, at his side.

That was in the days of Diamond's innocent youth. Diamond was only in training then for what was to come – his career as a full-fledged badmash, the terror of the neighbourhood. There followed a period when Diamond became the subject of scandal: the postman made a complaint. We had only to appear and Diamond would rear up on his hind legs, bellowing for blood. Nor was it just an empty threat, that bellowing: he had chased the poor man right across the maidan, making him drop his bag filled with mail as he raced for shelter from Diamond's slavering jaws and snapping teeth. The dog had actually torn a strip off his trouser leg, the trousers the postal service had given him for a uniform. How was he to explain it? Who was going to replace it? he demanded furiously, standing on the Das's veranda and displaying the tattered garment as proof.

Mr Das paid up. But even so, their mail was no longer inserted in the mailbox nailed to the door but flung into their hedge from afar. 'The dog is locked up, what harm can he do you through the door?' Mr Das pleaded after Mrs Das complained that she had found a letter from her daughter lying in the road outside, and only by luck had her eye caught Chini's handwriting. It was the letter that informed them of their son-in-law's recent promotion and transfer, too; what if it had been lost? 'That dog of yours,' said the postman, 'his voice heard through the door alone is enough to finish off a man,' and continued to use the hedge as a mailbox. Who knew how many more of Chini's delightful and comforting letters to her mother were lost and abandoned because of this? 'Is he a man or a mouse?' Mr Das fumed.

It was not only the postman Diamond detested and chased off his territory: it was anyone at all in uniform – officials of the board of electricity come to check the meter, telephone lines repairmen come to restore the line after a dust storm had disrupted it; even the garbage could not be collected from the Das's compound because it drove Diamond absolutely insane with rage to see the men in their khaki uniforms leap down from the truck and reach through the back gate for the garbage can to carry its contents off to their truck; he behaved as if the men were bandits, as if the family treasure was being looted. Charging at the gate, he would hurl himself against it, then rear up on his hind legs so he could look over it and bark at them with such hysteria that the noise rang through the entire neighbourhood. It was small comfort that 'No thief dare approach our house,' as Mr Das said proudly when anyone remarked on his dog's temper; they looked at him as if to say, 'Why talk of thieves, why not of innocent people doing their jobs who are being threatened by that beast?' Of course Mrs Das did say it.

Later, disgracefully, Diamond's phobia went so far as to cause him to chase children in their neat grey shorts and white shirts, their white frocks and red ties and white gym shoes as they made their way to school. That was the worst of all for Mr Das – the parents who climbed the steps to the Das's veranda, quivering with indignation, to report Diamond's attacks upon their young and tender offspring, so traumatised now by the dog that they feared to cross the maidan to the school bus stop without adult protection, and even had to be fetched from there in the afternoon when they returned.

'One day, Das, you will find the police following up on our complaints if you fail to pay attention to them. And then who can tell what they will do to your pet?' That was the large and intemperate Mr Singh, who could not tolerate even a mosquito to approach his curly-headed and darling baba.

Mr Das mopped his brow and sweated copiously in fear and shame. 'That will not happen,' he insisted. 'I can promise you Diamond will do nothing you can report to the police –'

'If he tears my child limb from limb, you think the police will not act, Das?' flared up the parent in a voice of doom.

The neighbours stopped short of actually making a report. It was – had been – a friendly, peaceful neighbourhood, after all, built for government officials of a certain cadre: all the men had their work in common, many were colleagues in the same ministries, and it would not do to have any enmity or public airing of personal quarrels. It was quite bad enough when their wives quarrelled or children or servants carried gossip from one household to another, but such things could not be allowed to get out of control. Propriety, decorum, standards of behaviour: these had to be maintained. If they failed, what would become of Bharti Nagar, of society?

Also, some of them were moved to a kind of pity. It was clear to them – as to Mr Das's friends in the Lodi Gardens – that he had taken leave of his senses where Diamond was concerned. When Diamond, in chase of a bitch in heat in the neighbouring locality, disappeared for five days one dreadful summer, and Mr Das was observed walking the dusty streets in the livid heat of June, hatless, abject, crying, 'Diamond! Diamond! Diamond!' over garden walls and down empty alleys, in the filthy outskirts of the marketplace, and even along the reeking canal where disease lurked and no sensible person strayed, they could only feel sorry for him. Even the children who had earlier taken up against Diamond – for very good reason, it should be added – came up to Mr Das as he stumbled along on his search mission, and offered, 'We'll help you, Uncle. We'll search for Diamond too, Uncle.' Unfortunately, when this band of juvenile detectives caught up with Diamond in the alley behind the Ambassador Hotel, they caught him *in flagrante delicto* and witnessed Mr Das's strenuous exertions to separate his pet from its partner, a poor, pale, pathetic creature who bore all the sorry marks of a rape victim. The children went home and reported it all to their families, in graphic detail. The parents' disapproval was so thick, and so stormy, it was weeks before the air cleared over Bharti Nagar. But it was nothing compared to the drama of Mrs Das's reaction: sari corner held over her nose, hand over her mouth, she stood up holding a rolled newspaper in her hand as weapon and refused to let the beast into the house till

Mr Das had taken him around to the tap in the courtyard at the back, and washed, soaped, shampooed, rinsed, powdered, groomed and combed the creature into a semblance of a domestic pet.

Mr Das bought stronger chains and collars for Diamond, took greater care to tie him up in the courtyard and lock every door, but when the season came – and only Diamond could sniff it in the air, no one else could predict it – there was no holding him back. His strength was as the strength of a demon, and he broke free, ripping off his collar, wrenching his chain, leaping over walls, and disappeared. In a way, the neighbours were relieved – no longer was the night air rent by that hideous howling as of wolves on the trail of their prey, and also there was the secret hope that this time the brute would not be found and not return. They hardened their hearts against the pitiful sight of Mr Das limping through the dust in search of his diamond, like some forlorn lover whose beloved has scorned him and departed with another, but who has not abandoned his bitter, desperate hope.

The Lodi Gardens clique, at the end of their brisk early morning walks round the park, seated themselves in a row on the bench in the shade of the big neem tree, and discussed Mr Das's disintegration.

'The other day I had occasion to visit him at his office. I intended to invite him to a meeting of the Bharti Nagar Durga Puja Association – and found him talking on the phone, and it was clear he was apologising, whether for the lateness of some work done, or for mistakes made, I could not make out, but it was a nasty scene,' said C. P. Biswas.

'His superior is that nasty fellow, Krishnaswamy, and he is nasty to everyone in the department.'

'Maybe so, but when I questioned Das about it, he only held his head – and did not even answer my questions. He kept saying "Diamond is missing, I can't find Diamond." Now I did not say it, but the words that came to my mouth were: "Good riddance, Das, my congratulations."'

The apologist for Das clucked reprovingly, and commiseratingly, 'Tch, tch.'

But one day, at dawn, Mr Das reappeared, holding a thinner, sorrier Diamond at the end of a leash while his own face beamed as ruddily as the sun rising above the dome of the Lodi tomb. He waved at his colleagues sitting in the shade. Diamond slouched at his heels: his last escapade had clearly left him exhausted, even jaded.

'Ha!' remarked C. P. Biswas, crossing his arms over his chest. 'The prodigal has returned, I see. And is he repenting his misbehaviour?'

'Oh, he is so sorry, so sorry – he is making up for it in his own sweet way.' Mr Das beamed, bending to fondle the dog's drooping head. 'He cannot help himself, you know, but afterwards he feels so sorry, and then he is *so* good!'

'Yes, I see that,' C. P. Biswas said out of the corner of his mouth, 'and how long is that to last?'

But Mr Das preferred not to hear, instead busying himself by making the collar more comfortable around Diamond's neck. 'Now I must take him back and give him his bath before I go to work.'

'Good idea,' said C. P. Biswas, tucking his lips tightly over his yellow teeth.

Diamond, who had been badly bitten and probably thrashed or stoned in the course of his latest affair, seemed to have quietened down a bit; at least there was a fairly long spell of obedience, lethargy, comparitive meekness. Mr Das felt somewhat concerned about his health, but seeing him slip vitamin pills down the dog's throat, Mrs Das grimaced. 'Now what? He is *too* quiet for you? You need to give him strength to go back to his badmashi?'

That, sadly, was what happened. By the time the cool evenings and the early dark of November came around, Diamond was clearly champing at the bit: his howls echoed through sleepy Bharti Nagar, and neighbours pulled their quilts over their heads and huddled into their pillows, trying to block out the abominable noise. Mrs Das complained of the way he rattled his chain as he paced up and down the enclosed courtyard, and once again the garbage collectors, the postmen, the electric and telephone linesmen were menaced and threatened. Only Mr Das worried, 'He's gone off his food. Look, he's left his dinner uneaten again.'

Inevitably the day came when he returned from work and was faced by an angrily triumphant Mrs Das bursting to tell him the news. 'Didn't I tell you that dog was planning badmashi again? When the gate was opened to let the gas man bring in the cylinder, your beloved pet knocked him down, jumped over his head and vanished!'

The nights were chilly. With a woollen cap pulled down over his ears, and his tight short jacket buttoned up, Mr Das did his rounds in the dark, calling hoarsely till his throat rasped. He felt he was coming down with the flu, but he would not give up, he would not leave Diamond to the dire fate Mrs Das daily prophesied for him. A kind of mist enveloped the city streets – whether it was due to the dust, the exhaust of tired, snarled traffic or the cold, one could not tell, but the trees and hedges loomed like phantoms, the street-lamps were hazy, he imagined he saw Diamond when there was no dog there, and he was filled with a foreboding he would not confess to Mrs Das who waited for him at home with cough mixture, hot water and another muffler. 'Give him up,' she counselled grimly. 'Give him up before this search kills you.'

But when tragedy struck, it did so in broad daylight, in the bright sunshine of a winter Sunday, and so there were many witnesses, many who saw the horrific event clearly, so clearly it could not be brushed aside as a nightmare. Mr Das was on the road back from Khan Market where he had gone to buy vegetables for Mrs Das, when the dog-catcher's van passed down the road with its howling, yelping catch of hounds peering out through the barred window. Of course Mr Das's head jerked back, his chin trembled with alertness, with apprehension, his eyes snapped with rage when he saw his pet enclosed there, wailing as he was being carried to his doom.

'Diamond! They will kill my Diamond!' passersby heard him shriek in a voice unrecognisably high and sharp, and they saw the small man in his tight brown coat, his woollen cap and muffler, dash down his market bag into the dust, and chase the van with a speed no one would have thought possible. He sprang at its retreating back, hanging there from the bars for a horrid moment, and, as the van first braked, then jerked forward again, fell, fell backwards, onto his back, so that his head struck the stones in the street, and he lay there, entirely still, making no sound or movement at all.

Behind the bars of the window receding into the distance, Diamond glittered like a dead coal, or a black star, in daylight's blaze.

Underground

❦

IN that small town, clustered around and above the bay, every third house was a boarding house, while hotels were strung out along the promenade, stolidly gloomy all through the year except in summer when wet bathing suits hung out over every windowsill and sunburnt children raced screaming across the strip of melting asphalt and onto the shining sands, magnetised by the glittering, slithering metal of summer seas. Sand dunes, dune grass, shells, streams trickling across the beach, creating gulleys, valleys and estuaries in exquisite miniature and shades of purple, sienna and puce. Boat sails, surf boards, waves, foam, debris and light. Fish and chips, ice-cream cones, bouncy castles, spades, striped windbreakers. 'Where can I pee-pee? I have to pee-pee!' 'Spot, come away! Come away, Spot!' 'I've cut my foot! Ooh, look, boo-ooh!' And a hinterland of blackberry bushes, rabbit warrens, golf links, hedged meadows, whitewashed, slate-roofed farmhouses – and the motorway flowing all summer with a droning, steady stream of holidaymakers baking in their beetle-backed cars.

The White House Hotel alone appeared to take no part in this summer bacchanal. Summer and winter, spring and autumn, it remained the same: an immaculate whitewashed cottage built of Cornish stone, with a slate roof, red geraniums in green windowboxes, and wrought-iron gates shut to the road. Not exactly the kind of place you hoped to find when you came to the seaside — it was not far from the sea, true, but had no view of it. Instead, it looked out onto the long, low hills, their green downs speckled with the white fluffballs of grazing sheep, in their hollows the kind of woods that sheltered streams, bluebells, yellow flags and dragonflies. Pretty enough, but not providing that sense of being at the seaside which was what you came to this little town for, a hellish drive in August.

Jack Higgins turned to his wife who had fallen silent and begun to take on a somewhat overbaked look. They had been imprisoned for far too long in that small, overheated car. 'What d'you think, Meg? Will it do?'

She shrugged her roasted shoulders under the thin straps of her yellow checked sun dress (it had looked very much crisper that morning when he had slipped his hands under those straps, heard them snap against her skin). 'It'll have to, won't it. There's no room anywhere else.'

That was true: they had already tried the hotels along the promenade, the houses clustered around the bay with their B & B signs. Every one had turned them away with the message: No Vacancy. It had taken them an hour to explore the possibilities and accept the inevitable.

'Can't we stop for a drink?' she had asked at regular intervals, like a querulous child, and as time wound on, it had turned to 'What about supper then? If we stopped for a bite, we could go further –'

But he had had enough of driving for the day. They had come a long way: it had been the hottest day of summer so far, and he would not tolerate another hour in that roasting oven of a car if he could help it. What he wanted was not a drink or a bite but a cool, shadowed room, a wash, a change and a rest. He knew that was what she needed too, even if she would not admit it.

So he compromised. He had pulled up outside a shop in town, hung about with rubber balls, flip-flops, spades and pails, and went in to enquire: in a town as small as this, surely everyone would know where there might still be a vacancy.

He was right: the woman selling fudge and postcards at the counter, once she had finished with the family demanding her attention and sent them off happily licking their lollies (four different flavours for four different children), asked, 'And what can I do for *you*, sir?' then launched into a description of every boarding house, bed-and-breakfast establishment and hotel in the vicinity. Jack could not see the point of so much information since every one, she assured him, was full. 'On a Sunday in August as hot as this, you get trippers by the *millions*,' she boasted, and watched him wilt and mop his neck with smiling satisfaction.

'So there's nothing? D'you think we might do better down the coast?' he queried bleakly, and found himself eyeing, with envy, a ginger-haired boy who materialised at his side, licking a lime-green ice.

Quite unexpectedly, and also eyeing the ginger-haired child and his dripping ice, though not with envy, she said, 'You might try the White House up the road that way. That's usually empty.'

'How far —?'

'Just round the corner, up from here, five minutes,' she said, and wiped her counter clean, defying the boy to touch it. He turned away but his place was taken by a group of young girls in tight, revealing jeans and doll-sized T-shirts. She gave them a testy look, her head waggling.

He wanted to ask her why she had not told him earlier of the one place that might be vacant, and how it was that a hotel so close to the coast could have a vacancy, but after opening his mouth he closed it again — two young girls with painted mouths and eyes were combing through a case containing lipsticks, and the woman loomed across to guard it.

He went out into the sizzling blaze of light reflected off the sea and sand to his car and wife, twisting the key chain around his finger.

Much as he yearned for the quiet and shade of exactly such a place in exactly such a green glade, he hesitated before turning into the driveway lined with neatly clipped conifers and evergreens. Slipping into the parking lot where the only other vehicle was a green Land-Rover, he turned off the engine rather thoughtfully before slipping out. 'Coming?' he asked his wife, bending in. 'Go and ask,' she told him sulkily, and it was clear this was not the kind of place *she* had had in mind.

Something made Jack run his hand over his hair, almost nervously smoothing it down, then glance down at his midriff to make sure his shirt was tucked in, before he crossed the parking lot and climbed the white stone steps between pots full of fuchsias to the front door. As he put his hand out to press the shining brass doorbell, he glanced upwards: something had caught his eye — the slight movement of a white muslin curtain upstairs. Someone had been holding it aside, watching him, and now let it drop.

Bob McTaggart turned away from the window, knowing he had been seen. He would have to go downstairs and open the door. He padded softly down the corridor, his footfall silenced by the grey carpeting. On either side of the corridor, doors stood shut. He glanced at each, at the number painted in blue on the central white panel, between the frosted glass ones: 4, 5, 6, 7. At the end of the corridor, on the landing, there was a small table with a bowl of dried flowers on it, and above it a mirror. He stood and stared at the reflection of the flowers in the mirror which had a blue frame decorated with sea shells. On its slippery surface, behind the solid form of the vase and the splayed stars of the papery flowers, there was a grey shape – his. He could only stare at the middle of it for so long, then he had to glance up, meet his own eye. Almost at once he glanced away, and went quickly down the stairs, to the corridor below. This was carpeted in blue, and its doors stood shut, too: 1, 2, 3. He passed them as if he were swimming by, with slow strokes of his legs, up to the front door. He felt the familiar response to the doorbell rising up his chest which was constricted, making air passage hard. He wanted to shout – and he was afraid he might – 'No! Go away! Go!' when he opened the door.

He stood with his hand on the doorknob – wooden, smooth, sensible – fighting back those words as he had done the first time they had had guests come looking for a room. He had just brought Helen back from the clinic that day, where she had had her check-up. He had been putting her to bed, filling a hot-water bottle, fetching her an extra blanket – warm as the night was, she was shivering – when a car turned in at the gate: it was a family of holidaymakers, the first ones of their first season as managers of the White House Hotel. Exactly what they had prepared for and waited for, and now there they were: the children hugging their bed-time dolls and blankets, the parents large and hopeful on the doorstep, impossible to turn away. He had been obliged to get a key from the office, open one of the shut doors into a pristine room for which Helen had chosen the curtains, the counterpane, the ruffles. The children bounded onto the bed, trying out its springs. The father wondered if anyone would give him a hand with the luggage, and the mother asked for a meal. He was flustered, he needed Helen, and she was lying in their room, on the other side of the living room, waiting for the hot-water bottle and the blanket he had promised her. But he needed to calm these people first, stop their invading the house any further. He thought that if he fed them, they would go away, retreat into their room, shut the door and leave him alone.

In the kitchen he bumped into tables and counters while opening cupboards, taking out bread, eggs, ham, cans of baked beans. He cut his finger on the can, blood ran into the tomato sauce as in a manic comedy show. He wiped both onto the clean teatowels. He and Helen had meant to take cooking lessons together: they had seen an advertisement, and enrolled – but there hadn't been time, and now all he could do was toast some bread, put baked beans on the toast, eggs in hot water, and he was failing.

While the toast burnt, the baked beans bubbled, sizzled and then subsided into a black crust in the pot, eggs split and oozed their gelid whites into the boiling water, he was reminded of the night when *he* had been the invader, the stranger, in another scene of confusion, chaos – strangely attractive – the night he had arrived in some desert outpost in Iraq where he was to spend three months, installing pipelines.

His firm had only just won the contract and he was the first to be sent out. They had told him there was an hotel near the airport where he was to stay till they built accommodation for all the engineers who were to follow. The airport had turned out to be a strip of tarmac laid across the sand which was quickly reclaiming it even as the small plane taxied down towards the long low barracks – he looked out to see it scurrying in busy wisps to overlay it. A windsock flapped in the hot white wind like a domestic flag. A man in orange overalls stood waving his two small flags at the pilot, a chequered scarf draped around his head and mouth. With a marvellous dramatic note, the sun, as orange as his clothing, but spherical and not oblong, was setting in a haze that surrounded him forebodingly.

In the barracks the Iraqi liaison officer met him with gold-toothed enthusiasm and insisted on carrying his bag, expressing surprise at its lightness and singleness, he could not tell with what sincerity. Tossing it into the jeep that waited outside, he had taken Bob McTaggart across what seemed an immense parking lot, already overlaid by the blowing sand, to another barracks, half-buried under the grains that had whirled through the air.

That was the hotel – hostel – whatever one might call it. It was clear it had few guests, if any. In fact, the doors stood open and its lobby was deserted as though, newly constructed as it might be, it was already abandoned. The manager, who was eventually summoned from some region beyond, led him down a corridor to his room. On either side there were metal doors, shut, numbers painted on them: 1, 2, 3 and so on. McTaggart pleaded travel fatigue as an excuse to decline the liaison officer's invitation to an evening's entertainment, then looked through the door opened for him and saw that although there was a wooden bedstead in the room allotted him, it was hardly prepared to receive a guest: the mattress had no sheets to cover it, only a blanket that looked like army surplus. A single unshaded light bulb hung from a cord to which flies had adhered themselves as though it were a candystick. On the discoloured wall a gecko clucked its displeasure at this intrusion. In the bathroom there was a plastic bucket and a tap but no drop of water. Yet the cistern above the toilet was stained with rust. At least it stank of hygiene – lysol, or phenyle, in quantities.

As darkness closed in, mosquitoes sailed in through the windows unimpeded because, although they were covered with wire gauze, the frames had wide cracks. He spent the evening lying on the mattress, trying to read the thriller he had bought at the airport for the trip. Then suddenly the generator stopped grinding – he had not even been aware that there was a generator till it did so – and the light went out, darkness whipped across like a blindfold. He wondered how he would get through that night: it promised to be very, very long.

Then, in no time at all – or so it seemed – the dark thinned into grey and the uncurtained window framed a new day, pale with sand. He was cold. He sat up and lifted the blanket about his shoulders. His mouth was dry, his throat scratched, and he felt he could not do without some hot water. He must get some hot water. None came from the tap so he went out into the corridor, huddled in his blanket, searching for the manager to help. The barracks – hotel, hostel – was as empty as the night before. McTaggart blundered into what was clearly meant to be a dining room – it had tables covered with white cloths on which flies clustered and crowded, and chairs with red Rexine seats. The only sign that meals had ever been served here were the plastic salt cellars, the bottles of ketchup, and the stains on the once-white cloths to which the flies adhered.

Seeing a swing door at the far end, he went out through it and found himself on a veranda looking across at a cluster of outhouses. They had to be inhabited: he saw a curl of smoke rise from a small fire. Standing there in the half-light, wrapped in his blanket, he could make out figures huddled around it. Eventually the fire flared up — it was just made of a few sticks in a tin bucket — and he saw by its light a woman who had slipped off her bodice from one shoulder and was nursing an infant at her breast. Beside her a man squatted with his head thrown back and his teeth bared in laughter as he clapped his hands: a small girl was dancing before them, in a red dress too long for her so that its waist hugged her knees and its hem swung at her feet, while her curls tumbled about her face and she struck her bare feet on the earth, swaying her small hips to the rhythm of her father's clapping.

He stared at them: the woman with her bosom bared for the infant wrapped in her shawl, the man's teeth and moustache and lips and eyes that glittered with laughter and love, and the small girl, her legs, feet and curls swinging to inaudible music. Shrouded in the dust and dimness of day before dawn, intermittently and sporadically illuminated by the small flames shooting up from the bucket, they had about them a quality so fragile, so immaterial and implausible that it could have been a mirage, a dream — a dream he might have had, in fact, of how life should be, how it might be, if it were different, and closer to what he so passionately, in such a rush of overheated blood, wished it were.

'Hallo!' he shouted.

The child ceased to dance, the woman hastily lowered her blouse, the man rose from his haunches in a flurry. Even the fire seemed to waver and go out. McTaggart, shocked at the dramatic effect his voice had had, wondered why he had shouted, why he had broken the fine glass pane of the mirage, and he wished he could withdraw, but the man was hurrying through the whirling dust towards him while the others in the tableau were receding into it. It was the manager, also huddled in a blanket, his face enquiring, and bewildered by the appearance of this intruder.

Suddenly angered, McTaggart demanded hot water, tea — chai, chai, he repeated, and heard his voice raised, loudly, like a caricature, a cartoon of a British colonial. And the manager's face, it became the other side of the colonial coin, confused, agitated, helpless in the face of these impossible demands, this infringement on his own life.

He remembered that moment now, that bubble of light in which those small figures had floated in the half-dark of dawn, his desire for it and his anger at it, the way he had shattered it with his voice, made all the fragments scatter and fly.

How strange, how very strange to find that he had changed places with them, so many years later, so far away, so inexplicably. He felt a sudden spasm grip his abdomen. He heaved with surprised laughter as he held his bleeding finger under the tap. He needed to tell Helen. Abandoning the ruined meal, he went into her room, and burst out, 'Helen, it's the damnedest thing — did I ever tell you — about that first time I ever went to —' and then saw her twisted to one side of her bed, her face contorted as she held back tears, and he stood stricken in the doorway.

Behind him, in the kitchen, the woman had appeared with a

bottle of milk she wanted to warm for her baby, and shouted out, 'Hey, the toast's burning! Mister?'

The two notes of the doorbell sounded through the house again – two small brass apples falling and rolling. Having seen the movement at the window, Jack Higgins had decided to persist. The late afternoon sun slanted out of the Western sky and sliced through the back of his neck. He mopped it, waiting with impatience and growing annoyance: he was going to get a room here, he insisted on having it, a cool room where he could wash and change and stretch out to rest, return Meg to a good temper before setting out to walk on the beach, find a pint of lager and some supper. He was not going to return to the car, to the road and the traffic, the heat and the lunacy of an August Sunday by the sea. His ear caught a sound – the brass bell-sounds had rolled up to an object, he heard a click – and he braced himself for the question he needed to ask, and the answer.

'Hello?' Bob McTaggart said, opening the door and wrinkling his eyes at the glare of the August sun, the red burn of Jack's face, the push of his belly against the wilted shirt, ready to enter.

'Have you a room for the night, for my wife and myself? We want to stop a night before we go on down the coast tomorrow,' Jack said quickly, even forcing himself to smile. The man in the door looked far from welcoming. In fact he looked as if he did not expect guests at his hotel or invite them and was astonished by the sight of one. Odd. Odd bod. Maybe that was why the woman in the shop below had seemed to recommend him with such reluctance. He narrowed his eyes, waiting for the answer.

Bob McTaggart shook his head very slightly. 'I'm sorry, I

have no room. Try the hotel up the road,' he said, and shut the door quietly.

There had never been time for those cooking lessons. The changes had all taken place so rapidly. Iraq, Nigeria, oil wells, installations, they had really occupied only a brief and negligible piece of his life, and receded as if blown back by the nuclear force of the news of her illness. When the smoke cleared, she had appeared out of it, pale and staggering, a victim, needing his attention, his entire, total attention. After the surgery, bringing her here to recover, he had felt the seams of his life, at first so drastically emptied by the news, filling out with his need of her, the comfort of her existence.

Perhaps that was why they had never made a success out of the White House Hotel: they hadn't really cared, couldn't really bother. They should have: they needed something to work out, to provide, when he threw up his job and brought her to the seaside, somehow believing they could flee the curse that had fallen upon them in the city. Like desperate refugees from the plague, they had also been pilgrims, voyaging in the belief that somewhere lay safety.

Could any place have seemed more of a haven, safe from wrath, than this sparkling inlet of sea, its tiny cottages like white pebbles clustered on the green clifftop, its innocent shops that sold ice cream and lollipops to holidaymakers, its fish and chips shops that filled twice a day unfailingly with the odour of their deep-fried fare? No sign of nightmare anywhere – no glare of lights, blank walls, beds like stretchers or pallets of torture, no gigantic machinery to swallow her out of sight, then return her drained of colour as of blood, exhausted, racked by nausea, only to have some nurse or doctor smile brightly across her corpse-like body and say,

'There you are! She's back!' as if summoning up a mother before her wailing child. He had not wailed, and Helen herself had said nothing, merely let him hold her hand and later, when she could, squeezed it.

At the end of that 'course of treatment', as it was called, he had made the decision, consulting her, of course, every step of the way. A new beginning in a new place. Somewhere quiet where they could pay attention to each other. What he meant was: pay attention solely to her, no distraction of going to work, catching trains, planes, going abroad. And after a few weeks in Mrs Bedford's B & B — Helen had not been able to resist that name, it made up for the lines of washing, the dishes in the sink, the sand on the floor — they had found the White House Hotel for sale. Although warned about its inauspicious lack of a sea view, they had bought it in the conviction that it would provide that shelter where they could be together and not be parted for a day or an hour. Its green hummocks of lawn, hedge, thickets and shade, its calm, its quiet, made it a kind of burrow for them to be safe in. In those early days when he needed to go and consult electricians and painters, or collect tiles or mirrors or carpeting, she had laughed at his reluctance to leave her. 'D'you think something would happen to me while you were away, *here?*' An unlikely setting for a nightmare, she had meant, but he had wanted to guard her, be certain that the illness could not approach her again, as if it were a crab scuttling sideways out of a crack between the rocks towards her.

He had not guarded her: he had failed to halt its approach, its invasion. There had been her pathetic attempts to hide it from him, to postpone the visit to the doctor and the clinic that confirmed its re-emergence; of course that had not lasted. Then she had tried to persuade him that people sometimes lived years in this condition – went into hospital, came back, had remissions; it was no more, she said, than a chronic cough, or asthma. She had gone on insisting that, while she shrivelled up on her bed into something smaller, more gaunt and emaciated by the day. Towards the end, not even a drive to the clifftop to look out at the sea was possible: they might as well not have been at the seaside.

Only one pleasure had been left and every evening he had carried her out onto the patio where their chairs stood side by side (those for hotel guests had simply been stacked and set aside along the wall). Settling her onto the wicker chaise longue, he had gone back to the kitchen for the bag of scraps, brought it out and sunk down beside her, holding her hand and not speaking. The blackbirds sang till it was dark. Down in the glen, the choughs circled over the elms till finally they sank down out of sight. Sometimes a fox cried. The sound of cars swishing by on the road dwindled and ceased. Sometimes there was a moon and sometimes a wisp of mist. They stayed very still, waiting, and then from the dark under the hedges around the lawn, the figures emerged, slipping along low on the grass, surreptitiously – dark, furry, with black bands drawn over their eyes as if convinced that these would provide camouflage. First the largest, heaviest, the one they felt to be the father, the patriarch of the set, and after him some that were smaller, more slender. Bob would empty out the bag of scraps a few feet away from the patio, on the grass, and they came sniffing delicately, hesitantly; but when they found the food there was a sudden tumble, a seething, a pushing aside and climbing over before they became engrossed in the eating, seeming to disregard the figures on the patio. Bob and Helen were not deceived; they knew they were being watched as keenly as they themselves watched, and sometimes one of them gave a shiver at the closeness of these dark, furtive creatures, the close sharing of the silent evening with the badgers.

Once Bob had almost spoken. Seeing two of them who had remained lower down in the garden, by the hedge, apparently playing games with each other, he had been on the verge of saying, 'What do you bet we'll see a whole brood of young ones in the spring?' and in time remembered the crassness, the cruelty of alluding to time, to the future, and he had bitten back the words.

There had been young ones in spring. The parents had brought them out to feed, moving disappointedly around the edge of the patio, sniffing. Bob had stood by the window indoors – it was cold, the nights frost-edged – and watched without moving. He could not bring himself to go to the kitchen and fetch them scraps. He had let them go hungry. Let them go and find the bugs and worms they live on, he'd thought, why should I feed them? What for?

Now he turned away from the door and walked down the tunnel of the corridor, its doors shut on either side. Going into the living room, he picked up and folded the newspaper that was lying on the table where he had thrown it earlier – *Cornish Panther Found to be Domestic Cat* read one headline – and tapped his cold, full pipe against an ashtray, then carried it into the kitchen to dispose of the ashes in the garbage can. The ticking of the clock was loud here, demanding to be looked at; he had always meant to change it for another, silent one. It was an authoritarian clock: telling him what to do, how to live. He probably couldn't do without it. He opened a cupboard, took out a loaf of bread, a tin of sardines. He placed slices of bread in the toaster, he fetched a can opener and opened the tin of sardines. Then he put all the ingredients together on a plate: they made a meal. He pulled up a chair to the kitchen table and sat down to eat. His eyes wandered restlessly across the table while he ate but there was nothing to meet his look: the blank face of the plate, the gleam of stove and refrigerator, all stationary, all featureless. He got up, went into the living room, fetched the newspaper and brought it back to the table, folding it neatly beside the plate so he could read while he ate: *Cornish Panther Found to be Domestic Cat.* He stared at the headline and the blurred grey photograph, stirring the crumbs on his plate for a long time. But eventually he had to rise from the table, wash the plate and stack it. Then he washed the sardine can before dropping it into the garbage can. He stood at the sink, vaguely aware that he had left something undone, and only after a long moment remembered he should have eaten some greens, that Helen would not have prepared a meal without some green ingredient. He considered washing some lettuce and eating that as an afterthought, but the prospect was so daunting he abandoned it.

Picking up the newspaper, he padded out to the living room again. Sinking into the chintz-covered armchair he waited for time to pass, looking out through the open door onto the patio where the garden sloped down into the glen. The summer evenings stretched so long, the daylight seemed never to fade, even after the sun was gone. For a while he wondered what he might do: mow the lawn, clip the hedges, trim the evergreens. Go into town and pick up some groceries. Or drive further out to a farm where he might get fresh eggs: that would be an outing, the kind of outing Helen enjoyed – small, trivial, undemanding. Just the sight of poppies blowing in the fields along the way, or the skylarks rising up above the meadows into the sky to trill, would give her enough pleasure to make it worthwhile. Then the fresh eggs would mean so much to her. 'We'll have a nice omelette for our supper,' she would say with the greatest satisfaction. To be satisfied with something so minor, so meaningless: how? He ought to have asked her, to have learned himself. It was not enough to have observed and envied her that innocence. With shame he remembered how, in his earlier life, it had irritated him to come back from Iraq, from Jordan, to have seen all that he had seen, and then come home to find her so placid, so *limited* he had thought then – and now it seemed more than he could ever accomplish. The poppies might have been beetroots, the eggs might as well have come in a box from the supermarket for all he was concerned. How had they brought that peach-coloured fuzz of pleasure to her face, a suddenly light, girlish motion of delight in acceptance?

He had tried, when summer came around again. Collecting carrot tops, greens, scraps, whatever he had, he had gone out in the evenings and scattered it out on the grass with abrupt, bitter gestures. You might as well have it, then, was what he wanted to say. They'd come creeping up, glancing at him nervously, snatching at the pieces, scurrying off with them. Did they notice that Helen was not there, his mate? He disliked them for not noticing, not caring. But the habit remained. It was something to do.

So now he gathered a meal for them, and scattered it on the grass, then settled down on the patio with his pipe, to watch the blueness well out of the hollows of the hills and slowly swallow the brightness of the daytime meadows. The hedges along the sides of the lawn swelled with darkness. A blackbird sang and sang as if to pierce right through the walls of his heart, then stitch them shut again. But the song became gradually less intense, less fervent, watered down, and finally disappeared. The choughs had already settled and even their grumbling and scolding had subsided. He sank back, his pipe unlit, wondering if his visitors would come tonight. He was tired – tired of doing nothing at all all day – and wanted to go up to bed, read a few more pages of the detective novel he'd bought in town, go to sleep. But he did not rise, he stayed there, one of those moments when movement became totally impossible having come upon him. He could scarcely breathe, the effort was beyond him, and he felt a weakness flooding through him like dark, or rain. He felt himself dissolve, become one with the silent evening, having no existence apart from it.

Then the white bands of their fur started up out of the dark, and their movements stirred upon the still lawn. The big one was leading, as ever, slipping closer to the patio by the minute, till it came close enough for him to look the creature in the eye. 'Hey, Brock,' he breathed out, the breath he had been holding back for so long that it hurt, as if his saviour had arrived. The creature paid no attention, its snout busy with a crust, but the slimmer, smaller one was slipping along through the dark and approached now. She came close enough to snatch at a bit of crust but, before she did, she too glanced in his direction, so secretively that the look could scarcely be discerned, and 'Hey, Helen,' he whispered, 'here, Helen.'

Having thrashed about for an hour, trying to sleep, Jack Higgins let out a groan of resignation, flung his arm over his head and pillow to touch Meg's head: the narrow bed made for a proximity that was far from comfortable on such a still, sticky night. Besides, the sounds of the revellers on the promenade below, screaming with laughter and curses, kicking beer cans along the pavement, made it seem like trying to get to sleep in a tube station. The window had to be left open to let in air and a streetlamp directly across from their window blasted the dark with its glare.

'Remember that odd bod in the White Hotel?' he asked Meg, who was yawning in frequent small gulps beside him.

'What was so odd about him?' she enquired, scratching at her neck and tossing her head about on the pillow.

'Bet that whole place was empty,' Jack murmured, 'and he wouldn't let us have a room. Now I wonder why.'

Meg did not seem to care. She jerked up her knees as if in anger. 'If that's so, he's got to be daft,' she said flatly, and resumed her scratching and yawning.

'Daft's right,' Jack Higgins sighed, thinking regretfully of that small green backwater, the shade of the tall elms across the lawn, touching the slates of the roof even in the blaze of afternoon. 'Daft as a —' and searching for the right word, he drifted into sleep.

The Man Who
Saw Himself Drown

❦

PAYING off the taxi in the portico in front of the hotel, he
went up the steps, nodded to the doorman, picked up his key
at the desk where the receptionist was talking dreamily on the
telephone, evidently to a friend not a customer, and took the
small elevator up to the second floor. Letting himself into his
room, he saw it had been cleaned during the day so that it
looked uninhabited: everything was put in its place, out of
sight, and the bedcover had been stretched over the bed and
smoothed immaculately. He tossed his briefcase into the
armchair – there, now the room knew someone had entered it
and made it his own – and went into the bathroom to wash. It
was what he had looked forward to all through the long drive
from the business centre to the hotel. In the creaking old taxi
with its seats slick with usage, going through streets where
people and traffic pressed in from both sides, and from front
and behind too, so that he felt they were being carried forward
by it. All the grime and soot of the city had seeped in at the

windows and under his clothes, filling in every crevice and fissure of his body. Now he luxuriated in soaping his hands and face and then washing off the suds and splashing his ears and neck as well. 'Ahh,' he sighed, wiping himself with a clean, rough towel. Ahh, now he was himself again.

He went back into the room, drew aside the curtains and opened the door which led to a veranda. Here there were wicker chairs and potted palms lined up against the white wall, and he chose one under a slowly revolving fan. Lowering himself into it, he uttered another 'Ahh'. But immediately he realised that he lacked something and had to get up and go back to the room to ring the reception desk and ask for a bottle of beer to be sent up. Then he went out onto the veranda again and settled down to wait.

He spent the evening on that veranda, drinking the cold beer that was brought to him on a tray. Gradually it grew dark. Small bats began to skim through the veranda and out into the garden that lay below, the crowns of trees filling it first with shadows, then with darkness. Small electric lights were strung from one to the next; these came on like buds opening all at once. He could see some of the hotel guests sitting in their light with drinks. Music was being played, but softly, unobtrusively, as he liked it.

When his business associate telephoned to invite him out to dinner, he made an excuse: he was very tired, he wanted to go to bed early in order to be rested and ready for the meeting tomorrow. Actually, he could not stand the thought of spending the evening in the company of the man who had been annoying him and irritating him all day. Although it might have helped to discuss their business privately over a meal before going to the meeting tomorrow, he could summon no interest in it at all: it seemed no more important to him than anything he had been doing for the last twenty-five years. He would go through the motions tomorrow but he could not pretend that he thought it important enough for him to give up an evening like this. He sipped his beer, ate the sandwiches and potato chips they had brought him when he decided not to go out to dinner, and contentedly watched the lights bob and sway in the pool of darkness below the veranda.

What he found he could not do was go to bed and fall asleep early, after an evening so relaxing and calm. He was not sleepy at all, in spite of the long, frustrating day at work. He was, instead, totally relaxed but wide awake. So he decided to go for a stroll, although the evening was warm and humid, telling himself a little fresh air would help to make him sleepy. Besides, he might as well take a look at some other part of the city before returning home tomorrow night.

The hotel was in the residential district, not the business quarter of the city. In fact, it had once been a private residence – a large villa, with a garden – and essentially had remained itself. So the street outside was as streets are in such an area: lined with trees, the lamps dim, few passersby and little traffic. The houses showed their lights through screens of trees, and over high walls. He whistled as he walked down those streets because he felt so calm and at peace.

Then he came to a great avenue where many lines of traffic moved. Here neon lights flashed, the cars' headlights beamed, and there was both noise and confusion. He waited on the pavement for the traffic lights to change, then crossed the avenue and found himself on the edge of a great park in which dark trees loomed as well as the pale bulbous shapes of the monuments for which this city was known. He had seen them by daylight, driving past, but they had seemed tourist sights then, both intimidating and slightly disappointing. Now at night, in the dark, they appeared more intimate, closer to him and his life. Again, he felt a happy calm and whistled, although he was also growing a little tired and his feet moved slowly over the dry grass. Sometimes someone would appear out of the shadows at his side, hiss at him, 'Psst! Psst!' and make suggestions or threats. He strode past them, refusing to stop and listen or be turned back by fear.

In this way he came to another avenue, also wide but with less traffic. The big lamps blazed on what was mostly empty tarmac. He crossed it easily and found it was lined on one side with boats, and that he had come to the bank of the tidal river that flowed through this city and that the tide was running high. A breeze sprang up, salt and sticky because it came from the sea but also murky and swampy because it was the delta. The sails of some big, flat-bottomed boats flapped with heavy, dull thuds against their masts. Small lamps burnt on decks, here and there, the wind making their reflections shiver in long snakes across the water.

He walked along and now his calm was ruffled by a sensation of adventure, of both fear and delight. Seeing the water glint, the waves heave, the boats lift and sink, he had a mad idea: what if he stepped onto the deck of one, untied its ropes and let the boat carry him up the river! It was ridiculous, at his age, to have this boyish, this childish urge, and he almost laughed out loud. He even clambered up onto the bank, looked at the distance between it and the deck, trying to gauge the length of a jump. His body impelled him forward but at the same time he threw himself backward to avoid the jump and the fall. He lost his balance for a moment, then righted himself, looking around to see if anyone had observed him. No, there was no one and he walked on, rapidly.

But he had to slow down and halt soon enough because a little further up, where there were broad steps leading down to the water, a group of people had gathered. From their attitudes and gestures, he could see they were agitated — they were crowding around something that one or two of them were dragging out of the water onto the bank. Water gushed from the object they lifted and from the men who raised it, and everyone was drenched. But they crowded around and called out in high, excited voices.

He didn't want to see, or hear. It was evidently a drama, and a moment ago drama was what he had longed for, but now he shrank back, ready to turn — he did not want to be drawn in. A shrinking and dwindling of his former urge overtook him, and he wished miserably that he had stayed back at the hotel, on the veranda, safely drinking beer.

But he had been seen. One of the people, a young man, called out, 'Police? Police? Will you go for the police?' Another, of a practical nature, shouted, 'Do you have a car? Can you take —?'

First he shook his head. Then he said 'No!' very loudly, 'No, no,' and thought of turning around and hurrying away. Just then the men who had lifted the drenched, streaming object from the river pressed past him as they laid it on the bank. He found himself, along with the others, in a circle around it, standing over it and peering down.

The body lying in the mud on the bank was of course sodden, and water ran from it in streams, but it could not have been in the water long, it was intact, and what I saw was a man five feet ten inches tall, with straight black hair that the river had swept off his face, a face that was square and brown, that had a cleft in its chin, a somewhat flat nose, and a mouth that parted slightly to show his teeth. Although it was dark, I could make out that the man wore a short-sleeved white shirt and the pants were of khaki material — that is, not very dark but not white either. He had taken off his shoes for some reason but still wore socks. The socks might have been green or black, I could not tell in the dark and the wet.

I stared at him, taking in every detail. Then I stared again, harder, and more details came into focus: the Tissot watch with the metal strap, the ball-point pen still attached to the shirt pocket. The face with the hair swept away from it, the flattened cheekbones, the cleft in the chin, the eyebrows black and heavy, the teeth uneven, crowding each other here, parted from each other there, and the glint of a filling. Every detail, in every detail, he was myself: I was looking at myself — after having spent half an hour, or an hour, underwater, sodden with river and mud — but it was I, in every detail, I. It was as though I was lying full-length, suspended in mid-air, and gazing down at my reflection below, soaked and muddy, but myself, I, after an accident in the river.

I do not know for how long I stared. But gradually I became aware that I was alone in standing stock-still, staring, that the others were all talking, hurrying away and hurrying back, bending over the man, touching him, and talking to each other in rough, rapid voices. Police, doctor, telephone, call . . . I heard these words, and then I saw them bend down and lift him up, three or four men putting their arms under and around the corpse, and together they hurried down the bank towards the lighted road. I did not follow them but stood on the bank and watched as they carried it away, shouting to each other in the dark.

It was only when they managed to stop a vehicle — or perhaps they had summoned it and it stopped deliberately —

and lifted the body into it that I became seized by agitation. Just as I had felt a few moments ago when I contemplated leaping onto the deck of a boat, now one part of me felt impelled to run after them, and plead to be allowed to go with the body – my body – and another part of me held back, pulled back with violence in fact, and once again I stumbled because I had made a clumsy, lurching movement, although whether forwards or backwards, I really cannot say. I think I may even have fallen on my knees at that moment; later I discovered the knees of my khaki pants were muddy, and that my hands were also dirty. By then I had walked away, in another direction. As I hurried along the lighted highway, I was in great confusion, wondering if I should have followed the body to the morgue and claimed it, or whether I was right to flee from the scene.

I did find my way back to the hotel – I remembered the address clearly – and I did spend the night in the safety of my room and my bed. Next morning I might have dismissed the whole event as a nightmare – a delusion caused by the unfamiliar scene, the darkness, the solitude – but when I was brought my tea in in the morning, and a newspaper, I tried to divert my mind from the horror of the night by reading the news while I drank tea and ate toast.

I found myself skimming the pages, regardless of what news was printed there, searching for a particular item that would bear my name. When I found none, I repeated the whole procedure in case I had missed it the first time. I repeated the act more and more frenziedly, as if I had to confirm what I had seen. I sent away the maid who came to clean the room. I did not answer the telephone which rang and rang at regular intervals. I stayed in my room all day, too afraid to leave it. I could not say what it was I feared, but I found myself trembling. When I was exhausted, I slept, but never deeply – I kept waking, each time in a panic.

I am not sure how long I stayed in the hotel in this state, whether it was two days or three. It certainly was not longer before the newspaper that was brought to me, and that I went through in such a state of panic that I nearly choked, finally revealed the news I had all along expected – and feared – to find: there was my name printed half-way down the column on page 7 in the local news. Of course my name is not so singular that I imagine no one else could possess it – there must be many men who have both the very common first name and the last. But it went on to give my exact particulars – the firm for which I worked, my designation, the reason why I was in this city – and ended by saying I had been found in the river at midnight, drowned. That I 'left behind' a wife and two children in the city of X. That no foul play was suspected.

No foul play? Then what was this that was happening? I had been declared dead. I was here in the hotel room, washed, shaved, ready for work, and I was informed that I did not exist, that I had drowned in the river.

For some reason, at that instant I found this comic, grotesquely comic. I think I laughed – I felt the ripping sound erupt from my throat, I assume it was laughter. How does a man react to such news – the news that he is no more?

Again I was in such a state of agitation that I could not proceed. I was to attend a meeting that morning: that was my reason for being in the city. But if I was dead, if my death was reported, how then could I proceed with my life and keep appointments and attend meetings and continue as though nothing had happened? My colleagues and associates would be thunderstruck to see me, even horrified. How could I submit them to such an experience? Or myself submit to it?

While I pondered over the best course of action to take, I kept to the hotel room. The telephone did not ring. Then it struck me that someone might very well come down from the office to collect my belongings, perhaps to go through them in search of some telling evidence such as a suicide note (if 'no foul play' is suspected then suicide usually is), and this threw me into such agitation that I decided to flee the room. For a while I considered packing and taking my suitcase with me, but then I thought the matter over and decided it would make my disappearance even more suspicious. If I left my belongings where they were, at least the death by drowning would remain plausible. So I hurried away without a single piece of luggage.

I have always been a conscientious person and it was very hard for me to slip out of the hotel without paying the bill, but when I went down the stairs to the hall, I was afraid the receptionist might have read the paper and seen my name in it. If so, he would be terribly shocked at seeing me. On the other hand, since he had not come up to examine my room or clear it, it would seem he had not. However, if I were to stop and pay the bill, he would inform my business associates of the fact when they came, as inevitably they would. The only course open was for me to leave, and leave the bill unpaid. This caused me a considerable amount of disquiet which I had to suppress as I hurried out of the lobby and into the driveway. There was a taxi idling there and I could have stepped into it and so hastened my disappearance but I stopped myself with the thought: 'Where would I go?'

Now I was truly perplexed. My previous life had ended, but did that mean I now had to construct a new one?

This is a hope, a fantasy many of us entertain in the course of our lives. What happiness, we think, to end the dull, wretched, routine-ridden, unfulfilling life we lead, and to begin on another – filled with all that our heart desires. Yes, but try to do that and you will find you are suddenly faced with hundreds of questions, no answers, doubts and no certainties. There is really no experience so perplexing. A new life – but what is it to be? And how to begin it?

I confess that I blundered around for the next few days – I no longer know how many – trying first one route, then another. Of course I considered escape; I knew it would be best to flee to another city, some part of the country where I knew no one, and no one would have heard of me or of my 'death'. But I found I simply could not embark on flight. A part of me was consumed by the desire to see what would happen now that I had 'died'. I even entertained the idea of going to my own funeral. It fascinated me to think I could stand beside a funeral pyre and watch my own body, my closest, most intimately known and familiar body, reduced to ash. In fact, it was the image that hovered before my eyes both in sleep and in waking. The only reason I did not follow this compulsion was the thought that I would be forced to see my family, who would naturally also be present, that my young son would come towards me with a torch to light the pyre, that I would have to witness his pain and my wife's sorrow . . . I knew I would not be able to control myself and remain 'dead' to them. Once when I was driving home, and had just turned in at the gate, I saw my son, then a small child, falling out of a swing that hung from a great tree, tumbling down into the dust. I leapt out of the car before it had even stopped moving – I simply sprang from it, abandoning it, in my rush to go to him and lift him in my arms and make sure he was not harmed. He was, slightly, and he was also to have several injuries later when he started playing cricket at school and bicycling and swimming, but that moment when he was so small and I saw him hurtling through the air into the dust like a bird was the moment that I felt our bond most intensely. Now that I was 'dead', were those bonds broken? Or would I become aware of them as soon as I was in another situation where they were tried?

I did not trust myself to have the nerves or the self-control required for such a bizarre experience, and so I stayed away, but all the time in a kind of anguish that made me clench and unclench my fists and often wipe the tears that streamed down my face. I could not even tell the exact cause of my anguish – was it for myself, the old self that had died, or was it for those I had been parted from and could not go to comfort?

I began to see that all of life was divided in two or into an infinite number of fragments, that nothing was whole, not even the strongest or purest feeling. As for the way before me, it multiplied before my eyes, the simplest question leading to a hundred possible answers.

This led me to blunder around in a state of still greater indecision. When the time came to an end that my body may have lain in a morgue, or possibly in my home in preparation for the funeral, and I knew – I cannot explain how, but I did with a certainty feel it within me – that I had been cremated and was no more, I was relieved. At least I ceased to see the scene of the cremation before my eyes in all its horrific detail – the smoke, the oils, the odours, the cries, the heat – and was able to put it behind me.

Yet I found I could not take the next step. I still felt caught, wrapped up in my life, my 'former' life as I needed now to think of it. It did not leave me free to think of what the next step might be. I was so absorbed in it that I can hardly provide any details of my existence at that time. I slept wherever I ended up – on a bench in the park, on a doorstep or a piece of sacking, or upon a sheet of newspaper. I ate whatever I could find; sometimes hunger made me see black and reel, sometimes I ate and was promptly sick. I know children followed me, laughing, down one street; on another, dogs barked and snapped their teeth at me ferociously and had watchmen come running out to chase me away. Somehow I escaped from them all, and mostly was left alone. Of course I must quickly have begun to look like a beggar, in just the one set of clothes in which I had walked away, and with next to nothing in my pockets.

It was in this state that I finally climbed onto a train – without a ticket for I could no longer afford one – and returned to the city where I had once had my home. By then I was reduced to a sorry state by being out in the sun and the rain, unwashed, mostly unfed. I felt, and possibly even looked, much as a lost dog does when it finally finds its way home, whipped, injured, frightened and hungry. Like that lost dog, I thought I would creep in at the gate of my house – I was still capable of such possessive thoughts – and go up the drive to the veranda, and I was certain, or at least ardently hoped, that my family would come out and find me, and treat me as they might a recovered pet, lavishing their attention and care upon me.

Somehow I did creep back to that gate, I did stand there by the hedge. I did look over it and see that the house was still standing, its verandas and doors and windows and roof, just as in the days when I had lived there myself. Even the tree by the portico – strange that I had never thought to learn its name – though it no longer had a swing dangling from its branches, was still large-leafed and shady, even if its fruit had never been edible except to the birds whose droppings spattered the driveway with white splashes and undigested seed.

So welcoming, so sheltering, yet I stayed out in the road, not even daring to touch the gate and unlatch it. The reason was that I saw many cars and people and much activity in that driveway and that portico. People were coming out of the house, carrying boxes, trunks, crates and cartons, and heaving them into a truck that stood waiting. After what must have been many hours, the truck rolled down the drive towards the gate. I made myself small against the hedge and watched as it drove away with the furniture and belongings with which I had filled my house. There was a moment when I thought of leaping onto the truck and going with my belongings to wherever they were being taken, but my body was much too weak for such acrobatic feats. Instead I huddled by the gate and watched as my wife – my wife! I called her that to myself, and yet the words already sounded strange now that I was no longer certain I possessed her and wondered how I could ever have imagined I did – came out of the house, dressed in white as a widow, with her parents on either side of her. They were all dressed in the colour of mourning. This distressed me greatly. I wished to run out and plead with them to change to bright colours once more. Had they forgotten how much I liked bright colours, had bought my wife clothes in every colour of the rainbow, and insisted my daughter wear reds and yellows and oranges? But here came the children behind them, carrying small boxes and baskets that contained, I felt sure, their most precious belongings. All of them came down the stairs to the portico where a grey car waited that I recognised as my father-in-law's. I watched them climb into it, and then there was a pause. Were they looking back at the house, saying goodbye to it? Or did they stop to think of me, whom they had last seen here? Then the car started up, quickly, with decorum, and smoothly rolled down the drive and came towards the gate.

Once again I pressed myself instinctively into the hedge. The last days that I had been through in the city had taught me to shrink, to make myself invisible, and so I did instead of springing out and standing there before them, in the middle of the road, and crying, 'Look, I am here! I have returned!' Neither the words nor the gestures came to me; it was as if they had been strangled inside me. How could I say them when they no longer rang true?

So the car passed by me, I crouched in the hedge, and none of those seated in the vehicle so much as turned their heads to glance at me. If only they had, surely those words, those gestures would have been wrung from me? Surely I would have cried out, at least to say, 'Please! Oh, please?'

As it happened, they did not. Not one of them turned to look back at the house they were leaving after so many years of occupation. Did they not feel any pang on departing? Their faces were all fixed, staring ahead as if into the future. Was that what concerned them – the future? Were they, perhaps, looking forward to it, eager for it?

And when I saw that, when I saw that they had a future, one that they looked forward to, or at least moved towards with resolution, I admit that I also felt, mixed with the bitterness of disappointment, a certain relief. It was as though I had at last shed them. My wife, my children, my house, they were all gone from me, and curiously, I did not feel bereft so much as lightened of my load.

The car disappeared down the road. Someone in a

watchman's uniform came and locked the gate. The click of the latch reminded me the house was not mine, had in fact never been mine; it had belonged to the company for which I worked but no longer did. It was apparent they had asked my family to vacate it and move. And they had, to my wife's parents' home in another town. She belonged there, she was returning to it. She had been mine, my wife, for a stretch of time that now was over.

After a long time of sitting in a state of sorrow and exhaustion, I left my house and, not wanting to walk on the streets where I might meet neighbours or friends, I went by small back-streets that normally only servants and peddlers used, and came to the river that ran around the outskirts of the city. This was no wide, grand river as I had seen in the city where I died, but only a muddy, slimy trickle that ran through a wide sandy bed in which washermen spread out the clothes they washed, and alongside which stood a few straw-roofed shacks housing I had no idea whom. By then it was evening and I stayed on the bank and watched as the washermen folded up the washing, loaded it on the backs of small donkeys and led them away. Small fires were lit in the straw-roofed shacks which began to smoke in a dark, smothering drift. A child with a pot came down to the stones beside the river and filled it, then turned and wandered away.

By then it was growing dark and I felt it was safe for me to make my way down unobserved. I took off the shoes that somehow I had retained till now and left them in the grasses by the side of the road, then walked down and across the sand, which felt gritty to my feet, and came to the water. It looked more like a drain than a natural stream but I was in such need that I bent with cupped hands and scooped up some water to first wash my face, then splash some on my head and finally even to drink.

I could not have drowned myself in such a trickle if I had wanted to. That thought led me to wonder, as I stood up on the stones and stared into the murky opaqueness of the water, if that was what I wished: to drown this self that had remained, to drown the double of the self that had already died.

But that self, my other self, the self that had had a job and a wife and children and a home, that self was already gone. I wondered what it meant, that death of my mysterious double. It seemed to me that I had died with it; I was so convinced of this that I was not able to resume my life. But was that the only possible interpretation? Once again I felt my mind splinter into fragments that whirled wildly in some great vacuum, and one fragment that I seized upon as another possibility was this: could that death have meant that my double had died on my behalf, that his life was finished, freeing me, my new self, my second self, to go on with another life, a new life?

I searched in myself for an instinct, an urge that would provide the answer. Was it to be death, or life? I remembered how I had once stood on a river bank – in how different a condition, how different a state! – and considered leaping onto a boat and letting it carry me down the river and out to sea, but now I felt no impulse at all, not even one that needed to be confronted and stifled.

It seemed to me that by dying my double had not gifted me with possibility, only robbed me of all desire for one: by arriving at death, life had been closed to me. At his cremation, that was also reduced to ash.

Then I was filled with such despair that I sank onto my knees in the mud.

At daybreak the child with the pot returned to the river for water. What he saw made him stop and stare, first from the slope of the bank, then from closer up, the stones in the shallows. When he made out it was a man's body that lay in that trickle, face down, he dropped the pot on the stones in fright. Its clattering rang out so loud and clear, a flock of crows settling on the sands in curiosity took off in noisy flight.

The Artist's Life

❧

WHEN Polly returned from summer camp, there was still some time to go before school reopened. She took to slamming out of the house after breakfast and wandering barefoot into the backyard, disappearing behind the garage and the bean vines to where the old car tyre still hung on a rope from the maple tree. For years forgotten, its solaces were now to be rediscovered – the twirling herself round and round and then, when she had wound herself up to the point of strangulation, letting go and allowing herself to unwind in an accelarating spin; the dragging of a toe through the scrubby grass as she pushed herself moodily backwards and forwards; the contortions of her limbs into and around and about the reassuringly fissured and pulpy rubber to act out the contortions of the inarticulate mind. Then there was the great canopy of the maple drooping down over her and around her in its protective tent of green, and the sighings, stirrings and scamperings that went on softly and unobtrusively within it, and the shade, almost chill, it threw across the sticky yellow heat of the last August days. She hung, trailed, twirled and rocked within it, her eyes narrowed under a dusty fringe.

With those narrowed eyes she was gazing back into the remarkable fortnight of the summer camp. It made her push out her lower lip, clench her teeth as she remembered the bliss, so unexpected, so unlooked for, that came her way as if in search of her, Polly, its chosen recipient.

That summer, in the tedious summer camp beside the dully glittering, reed-edged lake in the north, Polly had been chosen the hand-maiden of Art. A red-haired young woman who wore long, tie-dyed cotton shifts, and smiled cat-like through green eyes and moist lips, had chosen her.

Of course Polly had been introduced to Art as an infant. Of course the local school provided her – indiscriminately, as it did all children – with paint and clay and crayons, and she had made, as all children make, representations of her home and family – triangular-shaped father and mother holding hands, box-shaped brother in outsized shorts standing apart – as well as of daisies in a vase, and even a lopsided teacup or two, each of them intensely satisfying for a day or two, then desperately unsatisfying thereafter.

But what Miss Abigail at the camp introduced her to was Real Art: in her whispery, bubbly, disquieting voice she had urged them to 'paint your dreams – show me what you dreamed last night'. She had spaced the words, leaving great gaps for them to fill, and then sighed a replete sigh, as one might when overcome by swirls of incense or opium, when Polly presented a particularly lurid or mysterious painting – headless, shrouded figures in shades of purple appearing on the surface of a lake with large, many-pointed stars shining down on them out of a streaky sky, or purple pigeons swooping down out of a pink sky to light upon lilac roofs (Polly was very attached to the colour purple, and perhaps it was only a coincidence but that was the colour that dominated Miss Abigail's tie-dyed shifts too). For the sake of that narrowing of green cat's eyes, that slow exhalation of breath that spoke such volumes, and simply for the sake of staying close to that enchantingly incense-scented young woman with her flowing red hair and flowing purple dresses, Polly dedicated the summer to paint, letting others canoe, shoot arrows, roast marshmallows or run around working up a sweat like the damned and the demented.

She came home reluctantly, dazed into an uncharacteristic silence, with her paintings rolled up into an impressively long roll – Miss Abigail had insisted she always use large sheets of thick paper for her art. The family had been faintly surprised by what she spread out on the dining table for them; they turned to her with quizzical looks and remarks like 'Very nice, dear,' and 'Now what is *that* supposed to be?' making her roll them up again in offended exasperation, and carry them up to the attic where she spread them out along with all her painting equipment. She was determined to find herself a tie-dyed skirt, wear her hair loose, not in tight painful pigtails any more, and spend the rest of the summer drawing long strokes of purple and lilac paint across sheets of paper, humming the melancholy tunes Miss Abigail had hummed at the camp. 'And then my lover,' she moaned under her breath, 'left me a-lone . . .'

Unfortunately it was very, very hot under the attic roof, and in that thrumming heat of late August she would find her head spinning after a while. So much so that she was compelled to stretch out on a sheet of canvas and fall into a kind of stupor, struggling to keep her eyes open. Spiders descended from the rafters and spun their wavering webs, or dangled like aerial acrobats over her head. Seeing one unroll its lifeline and drop, cautiously and investigatively, closer and closer to the nest of her hair, she swatted at it, and upset a mug of water over a painting of a volcano spewing blood-red and orange paint. The water and paint seeped through several layers of paper, staining not only one but several other paintings as well.

That was when she descended the stairs, arms crossed over her chest, chin sunk, looking down at her bare feet, oppressed by the burden of being an artist. 'What's the matter, Polly?' her mother asked, 'got a headache?' and her brother jumped out from behind a door, with a 'Yar-boo!' that made her drop her arms, jerk up her head, then stick out her tongue and scream 'You – *pig*!' or was it, her mother wondered, aghast, 'You – *pigs*?'

It was then that the maple's drooping August skirts and the rotting rubber tyre hanging from its branch became the only option for her during the remaining days of summer. It was then that she discovered she could sail through the green leaves and the yellow air and be the artist without having to go through the sticky manoeuvres required by actual painting. Truth be told, she had no distinct memory of any of Miss Abigail's paintings, only of her loose hair, the long skirts, the whispering voice. She became convinced that art was not so much a matter of painting as of *being* an artist. Her eyes blurred, seeing not the dusty leaves or the scolding squirrels, the grass with its sandy or weedy patches giving it an undesirable patchwork effect, or her brother's face with its ginger freckles leering at her through the bean vines that sagged off the garage roof, but great watery sunsets, wild frenzies of blossoming plants, suns colliding with stars, wisps of carelessly cavorting hair, and 'Paint what-e-ever you dr-ream,' she sang to herself, stubbing one toe into the dirt and making the tyre swing upwards.

Unfortunately, the old heavy circle of ridged rubber could not be made to swoop upwards. At best, it dangled in its incurably pedestrian way, refusing to lift her into the higher realms where she wished to go. Those unpredictable roseate dreams were cruelly limited, encroached upon by the undeniable reality of the house, yard, suburb – enemies, all, of Art.

Although the suburb was as neat and trim as a picture (a *childish* picture, not the kind Polly had embarked on with Miss Abigail to inspire her) – white frame houses with black or green trim, standing in meticulously mowed lawns, neatly raked driveways, garages that housed two cars and had roll-up metal doors – there were those necessary but unsightly bits and pieces, too, that owners had managed to conceal with varying degrees of success: garbage cans with lids weighed down with rocks to prevent raccoons from tipping them over and spilling the rotting contents, washing lines hung not only with pretty skirts and coloured shirts but also with more unsightly items of apparel, and stacks of wood that had not been touched for many seasons and were slowly rotting where they stood. There was even an occasional sick tree begging for a visit from a tree doctor by dramatically holding up one blighted arm or exposing a wounded flank.

One of the most unsightly bits of the neighbourhood stood, shamefully, in their own yard, in the corner where the driveway curved away from the house and disappeared behind the lilac bushes that no one ever trimmed, so that it really was not visible to anyone else but to them, and then only if they happened to go past the garage and around the lilacs to the end of the drive. Normally it was only their father who went there, in winter when he was obliged by contract to clear the driveway of snow, because at the end of the drive stood a two-roomed wooden cabin with a condemned porch and a sagging roof that had been let out to their tenant, Miss Mabel Dodd.

Of course the tenant herself was visible, when she drove off to work in the gauzy grey steam of early morning, in her beaten-up old maroon Dodge with the grey paint showing through and flaking off as it creaked past the lilacs, fell into and lifted itself out of the deep ruts outside their kitchen window, scraped by the low-hanging branches of a thicket of lugubrious larch and spruce trees, and then cautiously edged onto Route 2, pointing towards Amherst. It was usually already dark when she made her way back at the end of the day, the headlights of the Dodge dragging through the leaves and grasses, leaving behind shadows. The cabin itself could not be seen from the house. The tenant spoke to none of them unless absolutely necessary and greetings were not: the mother had discovered that when she tried to greet her on their occasional, inevitable meetings in the driveway and there would be no reply. The father claimed he had actually had some conversations with Miss Dodd regarding particularly heavy snowfalls and problems with heating, but the children had not witnessed them and suspected him of imagining a relationship that did not exist, even so minimally. He would do that, pretend to be sociable when he was not.

When she first took up occupancy, the children fantasised about her, made up stories about her secret life as a witch. The first Hallowe'en, they had even gone around wrapped in bedsheets and with baskets on their heads, to chant 'Trick-or-treat?' under her windows. She had simply not answered the door. The children persisted: the car stood outside, after all. They pressed their ears to the front door, listening for a sound – and heard creaks, cracks. They peered through the grimy windows to see if they could spy a shadow or a light, and Polly, peering through a slit in the sheet of grey plastic that hung over the window, thought she did see something pale, wedged into a tall-backed chair in the corner; it was certainly not a light. It had the substance of flesh, but without any variation, entirely pallid from top to toe – or at least as much of it as Polly could see. And a faint swirl of smoke wound around it, slowly floating in the dark. When the other children began to push at Polly and ask, 'Can you see? Can you see anything?' she turned and elbowed past them, then leapt off the porch, swearing, 'It's a ghost!' All of them echoed, 'It's – a – ghost!' and Polly could not explain that the ghost had not been light and afloat as it should have been, but solid and fleshy and dull.

It was easy to forget that Miss Dodd lived there at all. For long stretches, they did forget. They built themselves a tree house one summer and sat on its uneven planks, dangling their legs and looking out over the sagging, crumbling roof of shingles that seemed a natural outgrowth of the earth. It was a long time since the walls had been painted and it was impossible to tell what colour they had been. Now they were the colour of dried blood, a boring brown. There was nothing that could be called a garden or a yard around it; in fact, it was a wilderness of ivy and scrub and some peculiarly vigorous ferns.

Polly was still humming 'Pa-aint just what you-u dre-eam –' when she slipped out of the rubber tyre and slouched across the grass to where the jungle spread in order to examine those

ferns; her painter's eye saw some promise in their furled and
unfurled shapes and tightly wound, or else exuberantly
unwound, clusters. There was something serpentine about
them, something you might come across in a dream. She was
barefoot, and cautious, as if she expected them to hiss and
sway, and when she heard sounds behind her, she snapped her
head around to look. But it was only Tom following, lifting
up his knees and plonking down his feet like an intrepid
explorer, a switch held in his fist in readiness.

Since the tenant was always out at that time of day, they
could explore at leisure, and what they found surprised them:
at the bottom of the mouldering backstairs that ended in a
tumble of rhododendrons were a stone head, bald, blind, rising
out of the ivy, its shoulders submerged in all the dark
groundcover, and other bits of statuary – petrified hands and
limbs pushing out of the soft mould like gravestones, or lying
scattered under the branches of the spruce trees. They might
have been the remains of a battle, or else ploughed up out of a
graveyard.

Polly and Tom said nothing to each other, but breathed
hard and noisily as they turned over and kicked at various bits
of stone and clay and plaster – mostly human shapes, thick
and clumsy, and some abstract ones that could not be called
squares or circles or anything at all, just contortions, blunted
ones. There was something disquieting about these ugly,
abandoned pieces that appeared to have been flung out of the
windows of the cabin, only one, the bald head, evidently
planted. The children, unnerved, were silent, as if they had
walked into an invisible spiderweb in a forest or come upon
bones in the wilds.

Polly thought of the yellow stack of *National Geographic*
magazines piled up beside the sofa in the den, with

photographs of steaming jungles, vast ruins, ancient idols tumbled from their pedestals and lying prone on the forest floor. She caught a wisp of her hair between her teeth and chewed on it. 'Miss Abigail at the camp was a sculptress,' she said. 'She made a ballerina out of plaster. She said she'd help me if I wanted to try. It was real pretty. Not like this stuff –' and she kicked at it, but not hard, being barefoot.

'But that ole Miss Dodd didn't *make* this stuff, did she?' Tom said, striking out with his switch at a flattened nose. 'Bet she got it from somewhere – some witch doctor, maybe. Maybe she does voodoo,' he growled; he'd looked through the *National Geographics* too.

'Voo-doo!' Polly echoed him, in an even deeper voice. They began making spitting sounds of condemnation. There was an unpleasant smell about the place too. As they came around the back of the cabin, they saw the cause of it: under the kitchen window lay a pile of refuse, household garbage, kitchen waste, simply tossed out and lying in a heap, some brown, some black, some wet, some solid.

'Ugh! Did you *see* that?'

'Gross!'

'Diss-gust-ing!'

'We better tell Dad!'

That evening they did and he allowed some wrinkles to work their way through his forehead, but only said, 'Guess the raccoons'll eat it up,' and went back to staring at the TV screen in the den: a sign he did not mean to get up and get involved.

For a while their mother did her best to make him do something about it. 'Think of the flies,' she urged. 'It's a health hazard.'

'Christ,' he said, turning red – he'd been looking forward

all week to this match. 'I've put two garbage cans outside her
door – what more am I supposed to do? Clean her yard for
her? With the rent she's paying us, it's not worth it.' The ball
game was coming to an end in a frenzy of waving flags and
blowing whistles. Frustrated, he got up. 'And that cabin isn't
worth more than the rent she's paying – we're lucky she wants
it,' he added. That was that, he implied, switching off the
television.

But their mother would not let it drop: the thought of flies,
and disease, was something she would not tolerate in her own
backyard. Finally she brought out an unopened box of
garbage bags and handed them to him, ordering him to take
them across to her. 'If she won't come out, leave them on her
porch. She'll have to get the message.'

He went off grumbling and they waited for him to come
back and report. He returned with a hurried gait, his head
lowered, and still clutching the garbage bags.

'Didn't you give them to her? She's there – her car's there
– I saw it,' began the mother, but he flung them onto the table,
muttering something about, 'You can't just go bursting in on
people like that,' and disappeared into the den.

'What do you mean?' the mother demanded, following
him. She stood in the doorway, questioningly. The children
could not see him, he had sunk onto the sofa, and it was
difficult to hear what he said since he had switched on the
television again, but they were almost certain – later, when
they discussed it, they found their certainties matched – that
he'd said, 'What was I supposed to *do*? She *was* there, she
opened the door – nekkid as the day that she was born. Stark
nekkid. Not a stitch. What was I to do – hand over the
garbage bags for her to dress in?' The mother quickly shut the

door to the den. Polly and Tom stared at each other till sputters of laughter began to erupt from them. Tom's sputters turned to spit. Then Polly's did. They dribbled their laughter till it ran.

By what had to be an odd coincidence, the next Sunday morning they looked up from their breakfast of pancakes and maple syrup, and saw the maroon Dodge come bumping slowly over the ruts past their kitchen window, then turn around the lilacs and disappear: their tenant had already been out that sleepy summer Sunday morning and was already back, this time bringing with her a visitor. She had never been known to have a visitor before. That he was a black youth whose upright, only slightly inclined head they had briefly glimpsed was equally extraordinary – in their neighbourhood.

After breakfast, the children edged out into the backyard before they could be caught up in any busy activity their parents might think up for them. They made for the maple tree and took turns at swinging in the tyre seat, then climbed into the branches to see if anything remained of their tree house. That was what they told each other – 'D'you think there's anything left of it?' 'Can't see.' 'Let's go look.'

There was still the platform although the roof and walls had blown down in the previous winter's storms and snowfalls, and from it they could look across the yard and over the lilacs to the cabin. What they saw there was the black youth, in oversized jeans and a military-looking shirt hanging out below his hips, wearing a baseball cap turned backwards, sweeping up the porch with a broom, then coming down the rotten steps to sweep that area. Then he returned to the house and they saw his head at the kitchen window, bent over what must have been the sink and taps.

It was mysterious, and unsettling. Had she heard them, somehow, discuss the filthy state of her house? How? She would have had to be a witch, hovering in the air above them, invisibly. And who was the youth? A guest? But no one had a black boy for a guest. Had she employed him as a cleaner? What was going on? Was he going to stay?

The last question was soon answered: before noon they saw the car going up the driveway and edging onto Route 2, the tenant with her great flabby jaw sunk upon her chest as she drove, and the youth on the front seat beside her, also in a sunken posture. There was no explanation for this unusual visit, this departure from habit — none at all.

And it was repeated the next Sunday, so that it seemed to be a new habit. Quite failing to keep their curiosity to themselves, the children disengaged themselves from the rubber tyre and the maple tree — Polly had also quietly abandoned the paint pots in the attic — and found games to play on the gravel of the driveway in front of the battered old cabin. Hopscotch — something they hadn't played in years. The black youth, coming down the steps with a broom and a rag, unexpectedly stuck out his tongue, then grinned at them. He started to sweep the dust and cobwebs off the walls and from under the eaves where they hung in swags, then started to wipe the windows, so long obscured by dirt as to make them opaque. Turning around suddenly, he caught them gaping at him. 'Dirty, ain't it?' he said conversationally. 'Ugly, too.'

They did not know how to reply. Ugly it was, and dirty too, but it was theirs. Was it a comment on them, and their lives, and status? Certainly the facts were undeniable and they said, uneasily, 'Yeah,' and 'Guess so.'

'Y'know what,' he added, 't'owner's ugly, too. An' dirty as hell.'

They retreated, shocked. The boy and his efforts at cleaning up the slovenly shack became even more mysterious. He was not a guest, then. So what was he – to their sullen, black-browed tenant?

'Oh, a cleaner, I guess,' their mother said when they told her of this exchange. 'She must have hired a cleaner. High time, too. Never thought she'd do it.'

'D'you think she heard us? She'd have to be a witch!'

But their father only said, 'Good, place getting cleaned up at last,' with as much satisfaction as if it were his own achievement.

Instead, a shocking event took place that did not result in cleanliness at all. School had reopened by then, and the children had forgotten such trivial moments of their summer. Tom was launched on his project of getting into the swimming team but finding it far from easy, and Polly was struggling to maintain her identity as an artist (she had taken her roll of paintings to show the school art teacher who had looked at them down her nose and said, 'Yes, well, we're going to be doing pencil sketches and still lifes this term'). The routine of catching the school bus, going off every morning, bringing back homework, was settling into its usual monotony. It was early fall, the leaves grey and tinged with yellow, like the beard of an old man, when one morning Miss Mabel Dodd arrived at their back door and stood, in her heavy boots, her battered jacket, her hands in her pockets, and her chin sunk into her collar, addressing their father. Their mother, when summoned, went at once to see what it was about. So did the children, at risk of missing the school bus, and there in the drive stood the tenant's car, at which she was gesturing. It was scrawled all over with what was obviously excrement, since it stank, and in excrement someone had written the word PIG across the front and rear window. Some of it had been smeared over the hood, and over the trunk. When they tore their eyes away from this mound of desecration, they went out, walked around the lilacs and saw the cabin with bags of garbage strewn all around it, across the steps and over the porch. Miss Mabel Dodd stood with them, huddled into her jacket — worn, they saw, over a pair of faded flannel pyjamas — surveying it with them. Here finally was something she wished to share.

After a moment, the mother, audibly gulping, said, 'I'll call the police,' and fled.

It was a great pity, but the children missed the police visit — the parents would not, absolutely would not, allow them to miss school. And when they returned, the police had come and gone. The car was gone, too. Nothing to console them but their mother's explanation — as if it could.

'They thought it might be the boy she hired as a cleaner in the summer. Maybe she didn't pay him enough. Maybe she said something bad to him, something mean.'

'But who was he? Will they catch him? Will they put him in gaol?'

'Oh, I don't think he can get away — he was one of the boys she taught — in that school for delinquents, in Holyoke.'

'She *taught* —?'

They might have known — mathematics, spelling, history, all those rigours took over teachers like terminal illnesses; it was what made them so dried-up, so impervious to life. They should have known all along. Only the word 'delinquent' added a novel element to that grim pattern — and Holyoke, the gutted red-brick tenements, the emptied streets, the boarded-up shops, the groups huddled in corners of playgrounds where no one ever played, that they passed by on their way to Hartford, to Springfield and beyond . . .

'Yes,' said their mother, cutting bread for peanut butter sandwiches without missing a stroke. The slices fell into pairs, like the leaves of books, on the wooden board, then were thickly smeared with the oily paste, rising to a mound in the centre, thinning at the peripheries, before she slapped the leaves together, two by two, and drew a knife through each pair, pressing down, then releasing each triangle to puff up and rise, ready for sets of teeth to bite into, as luxuriously as sinking into soft beds of warmth and sweetness. 'She's taught art there for twenty years, the police told me. Those kids, they must be real hard to deal with – most of them from broken homes, or orphanages, and some of them with spells in prison. Imagine teaching them *art*! Imagine *her* teaching them art! Poor kids,' she said, laying out the sandwiches in a plate in a layered, fanned pattern before them. 'Can you *imagine?*'

Polly's mouth opened to form a protest. Her lips formed the letter 'O' or else 'NO'. She wanted to protest, she was not sure against what, but against something that had been presented to her, interposed between her and what she wanted and believed in – something objectionable, inadmissable, an imperfection. How was she to protest, to deny? Her lips stretched to form the word 'How?' but then she broke down and what burst from her was a surprising, 'Oh, Ma-ma.'

Her mother looked at her, questioningly. What was she protesting? Polly had no idea. All she knew was disillusion. It made her stretch out and grab a sandwich, then bury her teeth into it, despairingly.

Five Hours to Simla
or *Faisla*

THEN, miraculously, out of the pelt of yellow fur that was the dust growing across the great northern Indian plain, a wavering grey line emerged. It might have been a cloud bank looming, but it was not – the sun blazed, the earth shrivelled, the heat burned away every trace of such beneficence. Yet the grey darkened, turned bluish, took on substance.

'Look – mountains!'

'Where?'

'No! I can't see any mountains.'

'Are you blind? Look, look up – not down, fool!'

A scuffle broke out between the boys on the sticky grime of the Rexine-covered front seat and was quietened by a tap on their heads from their mother at the back. 'Yes, yes, mountains. The Himalayas. We'll be there soon.'

'Hunh.' A sceptical grunt from the driver of the tired, dust-coated grey Ambassador car. 'At least five more hours to Simla.' He ran his hand over the back of his neck where all the dirt of the road seemed to have found its way under the wilting cotton collar.

'Sim-la! Sim-la!' the boys set up a chant, their knees jouncing up and down in unison.

Smack, the driver's left hand landed on the closest pair, bringing out an instant flush of red and sudden, sullen silence.

'Be quiet!' the mother hissed from the back seat, unnecessarily.

The Ambassador gave a sudden lurch, throwing everyone forwards. The baby, whose mouth had been glued to the nipple of a rubber bottle like a fly to syrup, came unstuck and let out a wail of indignation. Even the mother let out a small involuntary cry. Her daughter, who had been asleep on the back seat, her legs across her mother's lap, crowding the baby and its bottle, now stirred.

'Accident!' howled the small boy who had been smacked, triumphantly.

But no, it was not. His father had stopped, with the usual infuriating control exercised by robotic adults, just short of the bicycle rickshaw ahead. The bicycle rickshaw had, equally robotically, avoided riding forwards into the bullock cart carrying a party of farmers' families to market. Then there was a bus, loaded with baggage and spilling over with passengers, and that too had shuddered to a halt with a grinding of brakes. Ahead of it was a truck, wrapped and folded in canvas sheets that blocked all else from sight. The mountains had disappeared and so had the road.

Also the first cacophony of screeching brakes and grinding gears. There followed the comparatively static hum of engines, and drivers waited in exasperation for the next lurch forwards. For the moment there was a lull, unusual on that highway. Then the waiting very quickly began to fray at the edges. The sun was beating on the metal of the vehicles and the road lay flattened across the parched plain without a tree to screen them from the sun or dust. First one car horn began to honk, then a bicycle rickshaw began to clang its bell, then a truck blared its musical horn maddeningly, and then the lesser ones began to go pom-pom, pom-pom, almost in harmony, and suddenly, out of the centre of all that noise, a long piercing wail emerged, almost from under their feet or out of their own mouths.

The two boys, the girl, the baby, all sat up, shocked, more so when they saw it was their father who was the perpetrator of this outrage. Clenching the wheel with both hands, his head was lowered onto it and the blare of the horn seemed to issue out of his fury.

The mother exclaimed.

He raised his head and banged on the wheel, struck it. 'How will we get to Simla before dark?' he howled.

The mother exclaimed again, shocked, 'But we'll be moving again, in a minute.'

As if to contradict her, the driver of the mountainous truck stalled at the top of the line swung himself out of the cabin into the road. He'd turned off his engine and stood in the deeply rutted dust, fumbling in his shirt pocket for cigarettes.

Other drivers got out of and off their vehicles – the bullock cart driver lowered himself from the creaking cart, the bicycle rickshaw driver descended, the bus driver got out and stalked, in his sweat-drenched khakis, towards the truck driver standing at the head of the line, and they all demanded, 'What's going on? Breakdown?'

The truck driver watched them approach but he was lighting his cigarette and didn't answer till it was lit and between his fingers. Then he waved an arm – and his movements were leisurely, elegant, quite unlike what his driving had been, on the highway in front of them, maniacal – and said, 'Stone throw. Somebody threw a stone. Hit my windshield. Cracked it.'

The father in the Ambassador had also joined them in the road. Hand on his hips, he demanded, 'So?'

'So?' said the truck driver, narrowing his eyes. They were grey in a tanned face, heavily outlined and elongated with kohl, and his hair was tied up in a bandana with a long loose end that dangled upon his shoulder. 'So we won't be moving again till the person who did it is caught and brought to a faisla.'

Immediately a babble broke out. All the drivers flung out their hands and arms in angry, demanding gestures, their voices rose in questioning, in cajoling, in argument. The truck driver stood looking at them, watching them, his face expressionless. Now and then he lifted the cigarette to his mouth and drew a deep puff. Then abruptly he swung around, clambered back into the cabin of his truck and started the engine with a roar, at which the others fell back, their attitudes slackening in relief. But then he wheeled it around and parked it squarely across the highway so no traffic could get past in either direction. The highway at that point had narrowed to a small culvert across a dry stream-bed full of stones. Now he clambered out again, then up the bank of the culvert on which he sat himself down, his legs wide apart in their loose and not too clean pyjamas, and sat there regarding the traffic piling up in both directions as though he might be regarding sheep filing into a pen.

The knot of drivers in the road began to grow, joined by many of the passengers demanding to know the cause of this impasse.

'Dadd-ee! Dadd-ee!' the small boys yelled, hanging out of the door their father had left open and all but falling out into the dust. 'What's happened, Dadd-ee?'

'Shut the door!' their mother ordered sharply, but too late. A yellow pai dog came crawling out of the shallow ditch that ran alongside the road and, spying an open door, came slinking up to it, thin hairless tail between its legs, eyes showing their whites, hoping for bread but quite prepared for a blow instead.

The boys drew back on seeing its exploring snout, the upper lip lifted back from the teeth in readiness for a taste of bread. 'Mad dog!' shouted one. 'Mad dog!' bellowed the other.

'Shh!' hissed their mother.

Since no one in the car dared drive away a creature so dangerous, someone else did: a stone struck its ribs and with a yelp it ducked under the car and crept there to hide. But already the next beggar was at the door, throwing himself in with much the same mixture of leering enquiry and cringing readiness to withdraw. In place of one of his legs was a crutch worn down to almost a peg. 'Bread,' he whined, stretching out a bandaged hand. 'Paisa, paisa. Mother, mother,' he pleaded, seeing the mother cower back in her seat with the baby. The children cowered back too.

They knew that if they remained thus for long enough, and made no move towards purse or coin, he would leave: he couldn't afford to waste too much time on them when there were so many potential donors lined so conveniently up and down the highway. The mother stared glassily ahead through the windscreen at the heat beating off the metal bonnet. The children could not tear their eyes away from the beggar – his sores, his bandages, his crippled leg, the flies gathering . . .

When he moved on, the mother raised a corner of her sari

to her mouth and nose. From behind it she hissed again, 'Shut-the-door!'

Unsticking their damp legs from the moistly adhesive seat, the boys scrambled to do so. As they leant out to grab the door, however, and the good feel of the blazing sun and the open air struck at their faces and arms, they turned around to plead, 'Can we get out? Can we go and see what's happening?'

So ardent was their need that they were about to fall out of the open door when they saw their father detaching himself from the knot of passengers and drivers standing in the road and making his way back to them. The boys hastily edged back, and he stood leaning in at the door. The family studied his face for signs; they were all adept at this, practising it daily over the breakfast table at home, and again when he came back from work. But this situation was a new one, a baffling one: they could not read it, or his position on it.

'What's happening?' the mother asked at last, faintly.

'Damn truck driver,' he swore through dark lips. 'Some boy threw a rock at it – probably some goatherd in the field – and cracked the windscreen. He's parked the truck across the road, won't let anyone pass. Says he won't move till the police come and and get him compensation. Stupid damn fool – what compensation is a goatherd going to pay even if they find him?'

The mother leaned her head back. What had reason to do with men's tempers? she might have asked. Instead she sighed. 'Is there a policeman?'

'What – here? In this forsaken desert?' her husband retorted. Withdrawing his head, he stood taking in harsh breaths of overheated, dust-laden air as if he were drawing in all the stupidity around him. He could see passengers climbing down from the bus and the bullock cart, clambering across the ditch into the fields, and fanning out – some to lower their trousers, others to lift their saris in the inadequate shelter provided by thorn bushes. If the glare was not playing tricks with his eyes, he thought he saw a puff of dust in the distance that might be raised by goats' hooves.

'Take me to see, Dadd-ee, take me to see,' the boys had begun to clamour, and to their astonishment he stood aside and let them climb out and even led them back to the truck that stood stalled imperviously across the culvert.

The mother opened and shut her mouth silently. Her daughter stood up and hung over the front seat to watch their disappearing figures. In despair, she cried, 'They're gone!'

'Sit down! Where can they go?'

'I want to go too, Mumm-ee, I want to go too-oo.'

'Be quiet. There's nowhere to go.'

The girl began to wail. It was usually a good strategy in a family with loud voices but this time her sense of aggrievement was genuine: her head ached from the long sleep in the car, from the heat beating on its metal top, from the lack of air, from the glare and from hunger. 'I'm hung-ree,' she wept.

'We were going to eat when we reached Solan,' her mother reminded her. 'There's such a nice-nice restaurant at the railway station in Solan. Such nice-nice omelettes they make there.'

'I want an omelette!' wailed the child.

'Wait till we get to Solan.'

'When will we reach it? *When?*'

'Oh, I don't know. Late. Sit down and open that basket at the back. You'll find something to eat there.'

But now that omelettes at Solan had been mentioned the basket packed at home with Gluco biscuits and potato chips held no attraction for the girl. She stopped wailing but sulked instead, sucking her thumb, a habit she was supposed to have given up but which resurfaced for comfort when necessary.

She did not need to draw upon her thumb juices for long. The news of the traffic jam on the highway had spread like ripples from a stone thrown. From somewhere, it seemed from nowhere for there was no village bazaar, marketplace or stalls visible in that dusty dereliction, wooden barrows came trundling along towards the waiting traffic, bearing freshly cut lengths of sugarcane and a machine to extract their juice into thick dirty grey glasses; bananas already more black than yellow from the sun that baked them, peanuts in their shells roasting in pans set on embers. Men, women and children were climbing over the ditch like phantoms, materialising out of the dust, with baskets on their heads filled not only with sustenance but with amusement as well — a trayload of paper toys painted indigo blue and violent pink. Small bamboo pipes that released rude noises and a dyed feather on a spool, both together. Kites, puppets, clay carts, wooden toys and tin whistles. The vendors milled around the buses, cars and rickshaws, and were soon standing at their car window, both vocally and manually proferring goods for sale.

The baby let drop the narcotic rubber nipple, delighted. His eyes grew big and shone at the flowering outside. The little girl was perplexed, wondering what to take from so much abundance till the perfect choice presented itself in a rainbow of colour: green, pink and violet, her favourites. It was a barrow of soft drinks, and nothing on this day of gritty dust, yellow sun and frustrating delay could be more enticing than those bottles filled with syrups in dazzling floral colours. She set up a scream of desire.

'Are you mad?' her mother said promptly. 'You think I'll let you drink a bottle full of typhoid and cholera germs?'

The girl gasped with disbelief at being denied. Her mouth opened wide to issue a protest but her mother went on, 'After you have your typhoid-and-cholera injection, you may. You want a nice big typhoid-and-cholera injection first?'

The child's mouth was still open in contemplation of the impossible choice when her brothers came plodding back through the dust, each carrying a pith and bamboo toy – a clown that bounced up and down on a stick and a bird that whirled upon a pin. Behind them the father slouched morosely. He had his hands deep in his pockets and his face was lined with a frown deeply embedded with dust.

'We'll be here for hours,' he informed his wife through the car window. 'A rickshaw driver has gone off to the nearest thana to find a policeman who can put sense into that damn truck driver's thick head.' Despondently he threw himself into the driver's seat and sprawled there. 'Must be a hundred and twenty degrees,' he sighed.

'Pinky, where is the water bottle? Pass the water bottle to Daddy,' commanded the mother solicitously.

He drank from the plastic bottle, tilting his head back and letting the water spill into his mouth. But it was so warm it was hardly refreshing and he spat out the last mouthful from the car window into the dust. A scavenging chicken alongside the tyre skipped away with a squawk.

All along the road with its stalled traffic, drivers and passengers were searching for shade, for news, for some sign of release. Every now and then someone brought information on how long the line of stalled traffic now was. Two miles in each direction was the latest estimate, at least two miles – and the estimate was made not without a certain pride.

Up on the bank of the culvert the man who had caused it all sat sprawling, his legs wide apart. He had taken off his bandana, revealing a twist of cotton wool dipped in fragrant oil that was tucked behind his ear. He had bought himself a length of sugar cane and sat chewing it, ripping off the tough outer fibre then drawing the sweet syrup out of its soft inner fibre and spitting out, with relish and with expertise, the white fibre sucked dry. He seemed deliberately to spit in the direction of those who stood watching in growing frustration.

'Get hold of that fellow! *Force* him to move his truck,' somebody suddenly shouted out, having reached the limit of his endurance. 'If he doesn't, he'll get the thrashing of his life.'

'Calm down, sardar-ji,' another placated him with a light laugh to help put things back in perspective. 'Cool down. It's hot but you'll get your cold beer when you get to Solan.'

'When will that be? When my beard's gone grey?'

'Grey hair is nothing to be ashamed of,' philosophised an elder who had a good deal of it to show. 'Grey hair shows patience, forbearance, a long life. That is how to live long – patiently, with forbearance.'

'And when one has work to do, what then?' the Sikh demanded, rolling up his hands into fists. The metal ring on his wrist glinted.

'Work goes better after a little rest,' the elder replied, and demonstrated by lowering himself onto his haunches and squatting there on the roadside like an old bird on its perch or a man waiting to be shaved by a wayside barber. And, like an answer to a call, a barber did miraculously appear, an itinerant barber who carried the tools of his trade in a tin box on his head. No one could imagine from where he had emerged, or how far he had travelled in search of custom. Now he squatted and began to unpack a mirror, scissors, soap, blades, even a small rusty cigarette tin full of water. An audience stood watching his expert moves and flourishes and the evident pleasure these gave the elder.

Suddenly the truck driver on the bank waved a hand and called, 'Hey, come up here when you've finished. I could do with a shave too – and my ears need cleaning.'

There was a gasp at his insolence, and then indignant protests.

'Are you planning to get married over here? Are we not to move till your bride arrives and the wedding is over?' shouted someone.

This had the wrong effect: it made the crowd laugh. Even the truck driver laughed. He was somehow becoming a part of the conspiracy. How had this happened?

In the road, the men stood locked in bafflement. In the vehicles, the tired passengers waited. 'Oo-oof,' sighed the mother. The baby, asleep as if stunned by the heat, felt heavy as lead in her arms. 'My head is paining, and it's time to have tea.'

'Mama wants tea, Mama wants tea!' chanted the daughter, kicking at the front seat.

'Stop it!' her father snapped at her. 'Where is the kitchen? Where is the cook? Am I to get them out of the sky? Or is there a well filled with tea?'

The children all burst out laughing at the idea of drawing tea from a well, but while they giggled helplessly, a chai-wallah did appear, a tray with glasses on his head, a kettle dangling from his hand, searching for the passenger who had called for tea.

There was no mention of cholera or typhoid now. He was summoned, glasses were filled with milky, sweet, frothing tea and handed out, the parents slurped thirstily and the children stared, demanding sips, then flinching from the scalding liquid.

Heartened, the father began to thrash around in the car, punch the horn, stamp ineffectually on the accelerator. 'Damn fool,' he swore. 'How can this happen? How can this be allowed? Only in this bloody country. Where else can one man hold up four miles of traffic –'

Handing back an empty glass, the mother suggested, 'Why don't you go and see if the policeman's arrived?'

'Am I to go up and down looking for a policeman? Should I walk to Solan to find one?' the man fumed. His tirade rolled on like thunder out of the white blaze of afternoon. The children listened, watched. Was it getting darker? Was a thunder cloud approaching? Was it less bright? Perhaps it was evening. Perhaps it would be night soon.

'What will we do when it grows dark?' the girl whimpered. 'Where will we sleep?'

'Here, in the car!' shouted the boys. 'Here, on the road!' Their toys were long since broken and discarded. They needed some distraction. The sister could easily be moved to tears by mention of night, jackals, ghosts that haunt highways at night, robbers who carry silk handkerchieves to strangle their victims . . .

Suddenly, simultaneously, two events occurred. In the ditch that ran beside the car the yellow pai dog began a snarling, yelping fight with a marauder upon her territory, and at the same time one of the drivers, hitching up his pyjamas and straightening his turban, came running back towards the stalled traffic, shouting, 'They're moving! The policeman's come! They'll move now! There'll be a faisla!'

Instantly the picture changed from one of discouragement, despair and possibly approaching darkness to animation, excitement, hope. All those loitering in the road leapt back into their vehicles, getting rid of empty bottles, paper bags, cigarette butts, the remains of whatever refreshment the roadway had afforded them, and in a moment the air was filled with the roar of revving engines as with applause.

The father too was pressing down on the accelerator, beating upon the steering wheel, and the children settling into position, all screaming, 'Sim-la! Sim-la!' in unison. The pai dogs scrambled out of the way and carried their quarrel over into the stony field.

But not a single vehicle moved an inch. None could. The obstructive truck had not been shifted out of the way. The driver still sprawled upon the bank, propped up on one elbow now, demanding of the policeman who had arrived, 'So? Have you brought me compensation? No? Why not? I told you I would not move till I received compensation. So where is it? Hah? What is the faisla? Hah?'

The roar of engines faltered, hiccupped, fell silent. After a while, car doors slammed as drivers and passengers climbed out again. Groups formed to discuss the latest development. What was to be done now? The elder's philosophical patience was no longer entertained. No one bandied jokes with the villain on the bank any more. Expressions turned grim.

Suddenly the mother wailed, 'We'll be here all night,' and the baby woke up crying: he had had enough of being confined in the suffocating heat, he wanted air, wanted escape. All the children began to whine. The mother drew herself together. 'We'll have to get something to eat,' she decided and called over to her husband standing in the road, 'Can't we get some food for the children?'

He threw her an irritated look over his shoulder. Together with the men in the road, he was going back to the culvert to see what could be done. There was an urgency about their talk now, their suggestions. Dusk had begun to creep across the fields like a thicker, greyer layer of dust. Some of the vendors lit kerosene lamps on their barrows, so small and faint that they did nothing but accentuate the darkness. Some of them were disappearing over the fields, along paths visible only to them, having sold their goods and possibly having a long way to travel. All that could be seen clearly in the growing dark were the lighted pinpricks of their cigarettes.

What the small girl had most feared did now happen – the long, mournful howl of a jackal lifted itself out of the stones and thornbushes and unfurled through the dusk towards them. While she sat mute with fear her brothers let out howls of delight and began to imitate the invisible creature with joy and exuberance.

The mother was shushing them all fiercely when they heard the sound they had given up hope of hearing: the sound of a moving vehicle. It came roaring up the road from behind them – not at all where they had expected – overtaking them in a cloud of choking dust. Policemen in khaki, armed with steel-tipped canes, leaned out of it, their moustaches bristling, their teeth gleaming, eyes flashing and ferocious as tigers. And the huddled crowd stranded on the roadside fell aside like sheep: it might have been they who were at fault.

But the police truck overtook them all, sending them hurriedly into the ditch for safety, and drew up at the culvert. Here the police jumped out, landing with great thuds on the asphalt, and striking their canes hard upon it for good measure. The truck's headlights lit up the bank with its pallid wash.

Caught in that illumination, the truck driver sprawling there rose calmly to his feet, dusted the seat of his pyjamas and wound up the bandana round his head, while everyone watched open-mouthed. Placing his hands on his hips, he called to the police, 'Get them all moving now, get them all moving!' And, as if satisfied with his role of leader, the commander, he leapt lightly into the driver's seat of his truck, turned the key, started the engine and manoeuvred the vehicle into an onward position and, while his audience held its disbelieving breath, set off towards the north.

After a moment they saw that he had switched on his lights; the tail lights could be seen dwindling in the dark. He had also turned on his radio and a song could be heard like the wail of a jackal in the night:

> 'Father, I am leaving your roof,
> To my bridegroom's home I go . . .'

The police, looking baffled, swung around, flourishing their canes. 'Get on! Chalo!' they bellowed. 'Chalo, chalo, get on, all of you,' and they did.

Tepoztlan Tomorrow

🙖

LOUIS was let in at the big door by the old workman who had married one of the maids. He greeted Louis with becoming joy and affection, then led him through the courtyard which was quiet now, the maids having finished their work and gone. Louis had to duck his head to make his way through the rubber trees, the bougainvillaea, the shrubs of jasmine and hibiscus and plumbago that had tangled themselves into a jungle, leaving barely enough room to pass. The evening air was heavy with the scent of jasmine and lemon blossom. As he remembered, every branch was hung with a cage – he had memories that were still sharply etched of day-long screeches and screams that would ring through the courtyard and every room around it: the maids, doing the laundry at the water trough in the centre of the courtyard, crying, 'Pa-pa-ga-*yo?*' and being answered by twenty screeches of 'Pa-pa-*ga*-yo!' hour upon hour. But at this hour all the cages were covered with cloth and there was silence. A thought struck him: were they still alive? Perhaps they had all died: he imagined their skeletons clinging to the perches inside the shrouded cages, all beaks, claws and bones, dust and dried droppings below. 'Pa-pa-ga-*yo*? Pa-pa-*ga*-yo!' he whistled softly.

The house, to him, was a larger cage, shrouded and still. It seemed equally dead. There was one light on, deep inside; the other rooms were all shadowy, except for the shrine of the Virgin of Guadalupe in her gown of dusty net and tinsel, illuminated by the glow of a red light bulb suspended over her head.

The old man was hobbling along the dark passages as if he could see perfectly in the dark. Perhaps he was blind, and accustomed to it. Louis bumped into a sharp-edged table and suddenly all the picture frames on it clattered in warning, and a voice called out, 'Quièro es?'

As Louis approached the innermost rooms – actually the ones that fronted the street, but they could not be approached from it – the scent of lemons and jasmine in the courtyard and the heavy perfume of incense burning perpetually at the shrine receded and were replaced by an overpowering odour he remembered as being the distinctive smell of the house on Avenida Matamoros: that of mosquito repellent.

And there they were, Dona Celia on her square, upright, wooden-backed and wooden-seated throne, strategically placed so that she could look out of the window into the street and also, just by turning her head, into the house all the way down its central passage into the courtyard; and Nadyn beside her, poking with a hairpin at a Raidolito coil which was smoking ferociously and yet not enough to keep the evening's mosquitoes at bay.

Whereas Nadyn appeared stunned by the sudden appearance of a young man out of the dusk, and stepped back almost in fright, Dona Celia recognised him without a moment's hesitation. 'Ah, Teresa's son, eh? Louis, eh?'

Of course they were expecting him – his mother had telephoned, he too had spoken to them on the phone, all the while imagining it ringing through the empty house and the fluster it would cause in those silent rooms – but he was late, very late.

Dona Celia reminded him of this immediately. 'You are late,' she accused him. 'We have waited all day. What kept you, eh?'

He tried to explain, laughing falsely: he had hoped to get his father's car and drive up; he had waited, it hadn't turned up; he had made his way to the bus terminal but met friends on the way who insisted he stop, who delayed him. It was true, he admitted, taking off his hat and wiping his face, true that he had only managed to get away and catch a bus hours after he had said he would. That was how it was, he laughed.

Dona Celia's long face swung in the dark like a cow's. She shifted on her chair, wrapping her shawl about her throat – a shawl, on such a still, warm evening indoors; that too he remembered. All her movements expressed her displeasure. 'Well, we have eaten. Finally, we ate, Nedy and I. But Nedy will show you to the kitchen and you can help yourself before you go to bed.'

'Oh, is it bedtime?' he blinked. Already?

This was taken as an impertinence. She was not going to reply. A young nephew to speak to his aunt so, and tell her what should and should not be the hour for bed? Her face set into its deeply cut folds. Louis could hardly believe this sour old lady could be the sister of his laughing, plump, brightly dressed mother. A much older sister, it was true, and the daughter of their father's first marriage, more like a mother to her younger sister by a second marriage, but still, there was not the faintest resemblance. Perhaps it was the difference between the old family home in Tepoztlan which the old lady had never left, her own husband having entered it when they married, and left her there when he died, while Louis's mother had married into a family that lived in Mexico City.

Following Nadyn into the kitchen for a bowl of sopa tortilla she said she had kept warm for him, he sighed. Yes, Mexico City was very far, in a sense, not geographical, from Tepoztlan.

The bowl of soup Nadyn promised him turned out to be only one course of a succession of dishes she kept placing on the table and watching him eat his way through out of politeness, not hunger. She placed her elbows on the table, her chin on her cupped hands, and let her eyes wander. Why did she not put the light on? he thought querulously, peering into the dishes in the gloom, not even certain what he was eating although Nadyn assured him each time 'Your favourite.' 'It is?' he asked doubtfully, lifting a spoon and stirring. 'Of course,' she replied, 'we remember.'

What else do you remember? And what do you do besides remember? he wanted to ask her, bad-temperedly and unfairly, since she was telling him, in some detail, all the events of their lives in the time he had been away in the USA, quite as if she were sure he had heard nothing about them, living as he did in exile. As she mentioned this uncle, that cousin, or the other nephew or niece, he drooped over his plate gloomily, wondering if he dared light a cigarette and indicate he would not eat any more.

But now she was bringing out the pièce de résistance of the meal, carefully preserved in an ancient icebox that stood grumbling in its corner, and even in the gloom the colour of the jelly that wobbled in its dish was such that it made him cringe. 'Your favourite,' she challenged him as she set it, trembling, before him. How could he tell her that he had long since outgrown green and red jelly puddings?

'Only if you share it with me,' he said, inspiration having suddenly struck. By the brevity of her hesitation, and the eagerness with which she brought across a glass dish for herself, he remembered how Nadyn had always been the one with the sweet tooth.

'So, Nedy,' he decided to tease her, passing over all but one spoonful of the jelly to her, 'que hubo? Pedro – is he still around?'

She collapsed against the table, as if she had been struck. He had been unfair: he should have let her finish her jelly before bringing up the matter which he knew to be unpleasant, had a long history of being unpleasant. Now she would not be able to enjoy her pudding.

But somehow she managed to combine two emotions and two activities – and he watched with fascination as the woman with the long grey face and the two pigtails who sat across from him in her grey dress managed to spoon the sweet into her mouth avidly, relishing each chill, slippery mouthful as an armadillo might enjoy slipping slugs down its throat, and at the same time emitting an endless flow of complaint and grumbling, all bitter as ash, raw as salt. There was such a long, long history, after all, of Dona Celia's opposition to Pedro as a suitor, and her objections: that he was muy sucio, dirty, not fit to enter their house, and just because he ran a business in town. A business? queried Louis, was it not a truck? Oh yes, a truck was a part of it, how else was Pedro to deliver those bombas de gaz if not by truck, but did Louis know how the people of Tepoztlan now relied on those bombas for heating and cooking, how good, how thriving a business it was? It was not that Pedro was not doing well, or that he did not work hard. Then what was it? Louis enquired. Here she threw up her hands, then clutched her head, then clasped her arms about her, and went off on another tack: that of Dona Celia's stubborness, her adamant attitude, her rejection of Pedro's family – for how could she object to Pedro? No one could object to Pedro, it was his *family* – and here Nadyn became dejected, her mouth and shoulders and hands all drooped. She tinkled a spoon in the empty glass dish, making a forlorn sound: even Nadyn could not speak for Pedro's family. She had visited it, after all, and had to admit – and had told Pedro, too – that it was not the kind of home *she* had grown up in, *that* anyone could see. Pedro's home and Pedro's family could not be described as anything but sucio, not even by Nadyn. And she had not been given such a welcome by them either: they were not used to cultivated and aristocratic women such as the women of their own family, said Nadyn with a shrug, and their way of living – well, it was little better than pigs'. After all they had only recently made the move to Tepoztlan from the hills where they *had* raised pigs, turkeys, and scratched maize from the fields, but how could Pedro help that? He had worked hard to rise above that himself: only Mama would not see that, being of the old school – old-fashioned and stubborn.

Louis felt his eyelids weighted as if by lead with the repetitiveness of Nadyn's complaints. He could postpone the cigarette no longer. 'One day she will,' he sighed, without the least conviction, knowing as well as Nadyn that only over Dona Celia's dead body would Pedro cross the threshold of their home. His eyelids twitched with a sudden spasm of sympathy. People like Dona Celia took a long, long time to die — he did not need to tell Nadyn that: she knew.

He took his cigarette out into the courtyard to smoke. This was only partly in order not to offend his aunt's and his cousin's nostrils — they were used to the heavy coils of smoke of Raidolito and of incense but not of tobacco — but also because he could not help feeling absurdly hurt that Nadyn had not asked him a single question. Instead she had taken for granted that he would want to hear *her* news, *their* news, without the faintest suspicion that he might have some of his own. It made him feel ridiculously childish — no one ever imagines a child could have anything of interest to say. So it was with a somewhat sulky air that he strolled out into the dense jungle of the courtyard, thinking to sit down on a bench beside the water trough in the ferny centre and brood silently upon his own affairs before going in to bed. For a while it was as he remembered: the scents, the sound of water dripping, the howling of dogs in the lanes of Tepoztlan in voices more human than canine, so full of despair, desire and woe, and in the distance the wail of similar human laments on a radio, broken into by the raucous gaiety of a mariachi band playing on another, and overhead the night sky so deep and so dark that it was like being upside down and peering into a well. But very soon not only did the cigarette dwindle to its end and the bench grow distinctly cold under him, but what he remembered and what he reaffirmed began to have a profoundly depressing effect on his spirits. He saw the light go off inside the house, only the red glow around the Virgin of Guadalupe left throbbing, and then it became too much for him and he got to his feet and withdrew as if afraid this might be the stage, the setting for his life as well.

When he woke, much too late – the sun was already smashing in through the windows he had left unshuttered – it was to find the mood of Dona Celia's house unchanged. The courtyard was still uninhabited, there was no longer a team of maids and manservants to labour there, and although someone had drawn the covers off the cages, a number of them did turn out to be empty while the few that were inhabited contained only very aged, disgruntled birds that glared at him out of a single eye as he made his way past them to the main wing of the house for his breakfast, and did not bother to squawk a greeting or whistle back. In the house things were as usual. Nadyn appeared to have her arms deep in tubs or basins or buckets of housework, and Dona Celia, whom he went to greet, was seated as always upon her comfortless throne and, even if it was a summer's day and the sun beating up from the white dust in the street outside, she was wrapped in her shawl, holding it about her throat as if to keep every sort of danger at bay – draughts, chills, unsuitable suitors for her daughter's hand, whatever. Kissing her cheek, Louis actually found it chill to his lips – chill and mouldy, as if disintegrating.

But, while he sat over his café con leche and his pan dulce, he learned about the changes that had occurred during his absence. The house was no longer the barricaded fortress, the safe retreat it had been for previous generations of Cruzes: the fortress was threatened on every side. Dona Celia filled in the news into his left ear, Nadyn into the right, since he had noticed nothing for himself. In a way Dona Celia had herself brought it all about – and Nadyn was full of sharp little barbs to remind her – but having already sold off orchards and farmland lower down in the valley, she had finally resorted to disposing of bits and pieces of their own compound. Did Louis remember the row of sheds at the far end of the courtyard? Yes, he did and he also knew they had been bought up by an entrepreneur who had rented them to shopkeepers so that now there was an abarotte in one, a video parlour in another, a lavendaria in a third ... What was wrong with that? he asked, irritated. Not only was it old history but it brought in an income off which the two of them lived, so what was their complaint? First they brought change to Tepoztlan and then they complained of it. He pushed aside the basket of rolls Nadyn kept nudging towards him, and swept his hand over the dish of memelade about which a very large, fat fly hovered.

But now they were coming towards the true horror they had to face, its pit, its bottom: that end of the courtyard, round the corner from the row of rooms now kept shut, they had had a piece of land planted with avocados and lemons, did he remember? Well, they had sold it to a man who had come to them with cash in hand, and a suitably respectful manner of speech, telling them he wished to build a house for his family which had only recently moved to Tepoztlan. Being who they were – a shawl was fingered, a brooch nervously touched – they had not thought to question him regarding his profession or the size of his family. After all, if they had sold their land to him, they had no right to do so (and of course they couldn't wait to sell it and have the money in their pockets, Louis thought viciously; had they not always been money-grubbing, was not the whole family so?) and now they had for a neighbour a man who was a garbage collector by profession –

'What? *What* by profession?'

Louis' reaction satisfied them deeply: it set them off on an even higher pitch of complaint. The man owned a truck that he parked in front of *their* front door, often right under their windows so they could smell its contents, and even when the maid went out and persuaded him to move it down the street a bit, it left behind a trail of stray bits and leavings of garbage scattered all over *their* threshold. What was more, behind the high wall he had built around his piece of property before he had even erected a shack upon it, they suspected he stacked and sorted his garbage –

'What do you mean? He doesn't go and dispose of it, he *stores* it?'

'Yes, yes,' screamed Dona Celia and Nadyn together, in agitation: they were convinced, they had evidence, the maid had climbed up a ladder and peered over the wall and seen there all the empty bottles of agua purificada, the beer cans, the flattened cardboard cartons, that his family sat sorting into bundles for resale. And the family! By the rising crescendo of their voices, Louis knew he was in for a long saga. He began to squirm, to indicate that he was done with his breakfast, but they paid him no attention whatsoever, they were carried along by the tide of their indignation regarding the family because the man had not informed them that he had no fewer than seven children, boys and girls of all sizes, all in rags, and all day that was what they occupied themselves with, rag-picking, while their father drove around the town in his truck, loudly ringing a bell and collecting garbage to bring home to *their* doorstep. That was what the Avenida de Matamoros had come to, and there was no way of ignoring it: not only did the most noxious smell rise from the foetid garbage pile that was his compound, but day and night the place rang with the abominable music from the radio and TV – had Louis not heard it last night? *They* had been kept awake, always were. The man had not yet got around to building his family a house – well, yes, he had built some walls and a roof, but not a door or a window, not fit for habitation, yet a radio and TV had been set up in it to entertain the family while it sat sorting garbage. All day that ungodly music thundered through their compound – Dona Celia drew her shawl about her and shivered with fury. But the shawl was worn thin, no one cared how she shivered, such was the sorry state of affairs that Louis could see for himself.

He thought of rising from the table on the pretext of going and examining this den, this pit, this abomination, for himself but the two women were already onto the next disclosure of iniquity. Could Louis imagine such a thing: the garbage collector's wife, she put a table outside their door, *their front door*, every evening, and thereon boiled a tubful of corncobs and stood there, impudently as you please, slathering them with mayonnaise and chillies, selling them to passersby, as if Dona Celia were growing maize in her garden and posting her maid out there to sell it!

'I am sure that has not occurred to anyone who knows you, Aunt,' Louis said kindly, seeing her distress and beginning to feel a little amused in spite of himself.

'Yes, and what of all those who do *not* know me? Do you think Tepoztlan is the place it once was? Haven't you seen how it has been overtaken by hordes of newcomers, from Cuernavaca, from Mexico City, from God knows where . . . ?'

'It's now got a good road and good transport – it's more lively now,' Louis reminded them, although it was clear liveliness was not to them a quality: they would have preferred it a morgue.

'Yes, yes, lively – we all know about lively. Men come to our street corner to drink. All afternoon you hear them drink and gamble there under the bamboos, and by evening you may see them lying stretched out in the road, dead drunk – *so* lively has it grown,' Dona Celia said bitterly.

'Why, is there a bar now at the corner?' Louis asked with interest.

'A bar! I should think not! I am sure it is that vile woman – that pigsty owner's wife – who supplies them with liquor. Home-brewed. Oh, we would go to the police, inform them – but do you know what we can expect of the police of Tepoztlan? If people go to them with an honest complaint, and ask for justice, they are first asked "And how much will you pay us?" Do you think Nedy and I should submit to –'

Louis could not help laughing at the idea of his aunt and cousin visiting that most disreputable department in the town hall by the zocalo where policemen sat playing cards in the sun and their families cooked meals over open fires. 'No, of course not, Aunt – but perhaps Cousin Heriberto could go along –'

'Heriberto!' Dona Celia threw up her hands. 'That one! If you only knew –'

'I thought I'd go and visit him.' Louis scrambled quickly to his feet. 'Is he still at the old place?'

'*His* old place? You don't *know* what he did with it?'

Louis began to back out of the room. 'And – and Don Beto – I need to see him – about my thesis – ask his advice –'

The two women, still seated at the table, still seething and quite capable of continuing through the afternoon, found their audience disappearing at such speed that they were cut short in midstream. 'Thesis!' Dona Celia snapped as he turned and ran. 'I should like to know what thesis! Does he think he can deceive *us* as he does his parents!' And Nadyn shook her head exactly as her mother did, at the foolishness of such a notion.

Making his way out of the house, Louis ran into Teresa returning from the mercado, her market bag bulging with the

produce for the day's cooking. 'Ah, eh,' she greeted him
delightedly — how was it that his aunt and cousin could not
muster such a display? he wondered — and showed him the
vegetables she had bought to prepare for him, and the corn to
make the pozole, his favourite, she knew, then gestured at the
lane outside, making a face and warning him, 'Basura, basura
everywhere.'

It was as she said — the basura collector's truck was parked
outside the door, and bits of plastic bolsas and newspaper and
vegetable peel blew off it and littered the cobblestones. He
carefully stepped over them and, at the corner, where the great
clump of bamboos leaned over Dona Celia's garden wall,
there were the men she'd spoken of, leaning against the adobe,
their sombreros pulled low over their foreheads, and every
one with a beer bottle in his hand while empties littered the
earth around them. Louis could not help feeling amused to
find the town had crept up this far and was even daring to
assail his aunt's fortress. Perhaps one day she would be
brought face to face with the modern world. The confrontation would be worth witnessing.

He rounded the corner and crossed Avenida Galeana, then
started to climb the humps and hillocks of Calle de Cima
towards Barrio Santa Cruz, keeping his eyes on the ground
and picking his way from one cobblestone to another,
avoiding the trickles and runnels of drainwater in between.
The sun struck at the back of his neck and he wished he had
bought a hat from the woman with a stall at the corner on
Avenida de Tepoztlan, but it was too late to go back for it
now.

Up at the top, he paused by the church with the faded,
mottled pink stucco walls and tower that looked like
something made by a potter, then left out for decades in the

rain and damp. He had arrived at Calle Sor Juna Inez de la Cruz. He stood there catching his breath and remembered the times he had run up so lightly and eagerly, on his way to converse with the one man he held in esteem, the man whom he thought of as his mentor, and who had persuaded him to postpone entering his father's firm and go to university instead. He hesitated now because he was not sure if Don Beto would admire the way he was proceeding – Louis knew there was little cause for admiration – or even if he was still interested. It was such a long time since Louis had gone away to university in the States, and it was true he had been neglectful of writing letters to the old man or visiting him but, at the same time, if Don Beto were as he remembered him, then seeing him would surely give his work the impetus it required: lately it had foundered and stalled, leaving him wondering if he was really made for an academic career, if he hadn't better give up and enter Papa's firm. After all, his entire circle of friends appeared to have done just that, falling out of university one after the other, disappearing, then re-emerging as elegant young dandies, owners of sleek cars. Their social lives revolved on a higher plane to which Louis was invited whenever he visited from Texas but on which he felt like an interloper. It was one such invitation that had driven him back to Tepoztlan and to Don Beto: Marisol dressed in skin-tight pink silk and black lace, giggling, 'Paz? Octavio Paz and Hindoo philosophy? Oh, Eduardo, you didn't tell me your friend is a Hin-doo!' and making enormous eyes, while Eduardo called loudly from the bar, 'Louis? He was always a philosopher! Better give up trying to lure him, Marisol.'

He was resting in the shade of the church wall and thinking of that evening when he heard his name called and looked up to see his childhood friend Arturo parting the vines of a flowering squash plant on the hillside and peering at him. 'Louis, ola! Ola, Louis! What are you doing here? Thought you were in Houston or somewhere.'

Louis blinked up at him and answered as lightly as he could: he was not at all certain he liked encountering this apparition from a past life – schooldays, days when his family had all lived together here in the old house, before his father had taken them away to Mexico City. He and Arturo had played basketball together after school, in the court on Avenida Tepoztlan, looking out over the valley. Arturo had sisters he had been fond of, quite sentimentally, taking care never to betray those feelings when they were together. They had given him a present when he left, declaring he was sure to forget them otherwise. Actually, he'd lost it even before he got to Texas. He had not forgotten them, however, even if he had not particularly remembered. Now he shaded his eyes from the sun, chatting with Arturo, trying to say as little as possible about the university or Texas: it did not seem right when Arturo had gone nowhere, was probably helping his mama run the little abarrote down the street – what else was a young man with little school learning to do in Tepoztlan? But Arturo seemed not to share his embarassment at all; standing there on the hillside with his hands on his hips, he called down to Louis, 'You chose a good day to visit. Come along to the zocalo this afternoon – you'll see some fun.'

'What kind of fun?' Louis asked warily. His family had never approved of the fun boys could be expected to think up in Tepoztlan.

'Ah, it's a show we've put together, to show those bandits from the city what we think of them and their plan for a golf club –'

'A golf club?' It was the last thing Louis expected to hear. 'A club golfo, here in Tepoztlan?'

'That's right. It's a pretty place, no? Green hills, streams, nature – so why not come and spoil it all, make a playground for the rich so they can come up on weekends to play, and who cares if the green hills and the pure streams all vanish? Plenty of boys doing nothing who could caddy for them, too. But we're going to teach them a thing or two – we're putting up a real fight. Come along for the show – you'll meet the old gang.'

Louis wondered who the others were who had stayed back and were now members of this curious group he had never heard of, and even Dona Celia had not mentioned in her zeal to bring him up to date. He raised his hand in a wave, promising to come along 'after I've been to see Don Beto. He still lives up this way, doesn't he?'

Arturo beamed down at him. 'Oh yes, where would he go? He'll die here under Tepozteco – he's willing to die for the movement, you know. Just ask him about it.'

It was not at all what Louis expected to talk about to the old scholar, but the conversation with Arturo left him uncertain of what he might and might not find. Don Beto's house was exactly as he remembered it, built into the hillside under the forests and crags on which the small pyramid of the Aztec god Tepoztecatl stood perched, and invisible from the road and the wrought-iron gate. The rusty, cracked bell still hung from the branch of a mango tree, its rope draped casually over the gate for visitors to pull. Beyond, he could see the ruins of the former house, the one Don Beto had grown up in, at the back of the grassed-over cobbles of the courtyard, only one step and a broken arch left standing with a ruined wall for a backdrop. A canvas hung on that wall, incongruously – a painting of underwater blues and greens with piscine shapes faint in its wash. A piece of clay moulded into a curious shell shape lay on the step.

It certainly seemed like a gateway to the past, and Louis gave the rope a tug. Immediately a dog sounded a warning howl but did not make an appearance. Eventually Don Beto's daughter, Marta, came hurrying down the path between the avocado and citrus trees that grew at the back. She did not recognise Louis at first, and pushed a strand of grey hair out of her eyes to peer at the figure on the other side of the gate, but when he greeted her she opened the gate, shook his hand, remembering, smiling. What did she remember of him, Louis wondered.

'You didn't recognise me,' he complained.

'Oh, we are growing old, old – our memories are going,' she laughed, making an excuse.

'But still painting,' he said, gesturing towards the canvas on the wall and the shell sculpture on the step as they passed around to the back of the ruin and faced the house that Don Beto had moved into after his wife's death, nothing more than a small cube of concrete, weathered and mildewed, but a veranda in front where flowers grew in rusty old jalapeno cans.

She preceded him into the house from which she fetched her father out onto the veranda. (Was this town peopled by ageing daughters taking care of their aged parents? Louis wondered.) Don Beto was more bent than before, like a woodland goblin, with a face like a knot in an ancient tree, and he had a stick like a twisted root to help him move. Both his daughter and Louis tried to help him settle into a chair but he waved them away and perched on a bench, insisting that Louis have the chair instead. This produced in Louis a discomfort that lasted throughout his visit. Don Beto, unlike everybody else he had met so far, questioned him closely on his life at the university in Houston, on how work was progressing on his thesis, showing the same intense interest in what Louis was doing as he had always had. Louis had corresponded with him over the years and Don Beto had recommended books and writers to him all along but, to Louis' disappointment, he appeared not to have any suggestions to make now. For such a young man to be paid such attention by an old scholar had been a heady experience and it had led Louis to believe he could and should go to university and pursue a scholarly life himself, but now he sensed a certain remoteness in Don Beto, as though this pursuit was not a joint one as Louis had fondly imagined. It made him feel the loneliness of academic labour, the hardness of such a pursuit.

Marta brought them té de manzanilla in pretty cups, and a plate of pastries. Then, as they sat crumbling the pastries with their fingers and watching out of the corners of their eyes a minute hummingbird hover over a plate-sized hibiscus in a pot, Don Beto changed the subject abruptly, and made a wholly unexpected suggestion: perhaps Louis should turn his mind, temporarily of course, to another kind of writing. Polemical. Why not use his pen and his gifts to address the matter that concerned all of them so urgently? And what was that matter? Ah, had he not heard of the club golfo that a consortium of wealthy developers wished to create here, having robbed the country of enough and now having to find ways to spend that wealth, here in this unlikely, unsuitable setting of Tepoztlan, drawn as everyone was to its mountains, its sweet water, its flora and fauna, its allure. . .. He gestured passionately; the hummingbird fled.

Stillness

        not on the branch

in the air

    Not in the air

in the moment

        hummingbird

'Is this true?' asked Louis. 'I did hear — from Arturo —'
'You have heard? You *have*?' Don Beto questioned, and
seemed astonished that Louis had heard and yet not spoken of
it, or acted. 'Of this scandal? Then you must inform the world
of it, you must turn your pen into a sword and fight. . . .' The
old man lifted his hand from the knob of his walking stick and
held it up in the air, steady with command.

Louis left his crumbled pastry uneaten on his plate. Don
Beto was filling his ears with facts and statistics now, his voice
rising to a high pencil-squeak of indignation as he detailed the
losses such a project would create, the losses to what made
Tepoztlan such a treasure — no, not in the eyes of the world
that saw it as poor and backward, a place that should think
itself lucky to be chosen for 'development', with the money
such a club would bring in — but to what those who lived here
knew to be its wealth . . . and as he spoke of the environment
and its endangered condition, it was as if all the old interests
they had shared had been swept aside to make room for what
was evidently now the old man's consuming passion. Once
when Don Beto paused, Louis ventured to ask, 'And are you
writing poetry, Don Beto? Have you written any verse
recently?' only to see Don Beto set his mouth firmly and
dismiss it with a wave. 'I write what my young friends need,
in language that people can read and understand. Not poetry,

no,' abandoning what he had spent a lifetime on, and towards
which he had directed Louis.

Still bemused by Don Beto's — the unworldly, retiring,
scholarly Don Beto — actually having suggested he go in for
journalism instead of poetry, and all in the name of opposing a
golf club, Louis wandered down to the zocalo in the sun-
struck heat of the afternoon, wondering if he would find
anyone there at all.

In spite of Dona Celia's complaints, he found the town
exactly as he remembered it. Visitors from Cuernavaca and
Mexico City were still pouring in for the Sunday market as
they had always done, in their holiday clothes, to fill the
restaurants from which music loudly rollicked. In the zocalo,
he was sure the old couple selling pottery, their own faces as
brown and seamed and cracked as if fashioned from clay, were
the same he had always seen seated on a mat under the rubber
tree; there were the same elderly people eagerly buying herbs
and roots and seeds from the herbalist to cure them of gout,
insomnia, obesity and fits, impotence and urinary problems;
chillies hung in dark, leathery bunches that still set him
sneezing; the florist continued to decorate his potted cacti with
tiny paper flowers, and in the food stalls pans sizzled and
steamed and large curs prowled around the customers' feet in
the hope of scraps.

Louis remembered all that but somehow, after his visit to
Don Beto, he was not content simply to plunge back into it
and wallow in nostalgia. Instead, he drifted towards the big
marquee of blue plastic that had been set up in between the
town hall and the bandstand, the recording and amplifying
systems that were being unloaded and attached, and the
crowds gathering around it, some chewing on corn cobs and

others licking helados. On the steps of the post office he could see some of the young men he had known. Arturo was there, in the same striped T-shirt he had worn in the morning but with the addition of a baseball cap. Reluctant to go up to him, Louis lingered to read the legends on the banners flying everywhere – Puebla contra Fascism! Tierra del Morte! – and study the lurid murals that had been painted on the town hall walls: a rubicund golfer with a tail protruding from his golf pants and hooves in place of shoes, his caddy a grinning imp with pointed ears and a forked tail, together facing a group of peasants huddled in blankets, dark, weary and watchful. In another, over the shoe stall with its rows of huaraches, rufescent golfers sported golf clubs and grinningly molested frightened young women whose blouses had been torn off their breasts. Every one of the rubber and laurel trees in the little park around the bandstand, and every pillar of the post office, had smaller, printed posters pasted on them. Several depicted frogs, squirrels, butterflies and birds, each saying 'No' to the golf club in a different language: Niet! Nein! Na! Non!

Now the first strains of an amplified guitar rang out. People dropped the huaraches and sombreros they were examining, got up from around the roasted corn cob stalls, came out of the ice-cream parlours and cafés, and began to gather under the marquee. Louis strolled across as casually as he could, but when he saw who was playing the guitar and teaching the audience the lines he had composed 'for Tepoztlan', his assumed composure fell apart: it was Alejandro, who had been in school with him and Arturo, and had been known for his passion for fireworks, whose ambition it had been to launch a fire balloon which, once aloft, would release a burst of rockets. Now he was standing in front of a microphone in jeans and a black tank shirt, his head shaved on all sides, leaving one cornrow to grow along the centre where it stood in jagged peaks, dyed a fiery red. When he called out a line:

'Leave me my streams, leave me my hills,'

the crowd echoed him:

'Leave me my streams, leave me my hills,'

and then joined him in the refrain:

'Leave me my paradise, Tepoztlan.'

Louis fell back, allowing a party of curious tourists to edge up in front of him, in the hope they would conceal him from Alejandro. But of course Alejandro was not looking at him — he was plucking his guitar with his eyes closed and his head thrown back as he sang:

'Who dares to come and steal
My paradise, Tepoztlan?'

Someone was going around selling tapes of, presumably, Alejandro's songs. A young woman in a flowered skirt circled the crowds with a straw hat outstretched, collecting donations. She smiled into Louis' face: hers was like a ripe peach, so round and sweet. He dug into his pockets and brought out a crumpled note for her.

Now Alejandro was waving at the crowd and turning to run back up the post office steps and vanish among his friends there while another figure leapt into their midst: a lithe young man dressed entirely in black but with his pants cut off at the knees and his shirt open on his chest. In his hands he held an empty rum bottle and with it he performed a dance of a kind Louis had never seen in the clubs and parties to which he had been. He could hardly maintain his compoure as he watched the man crouch, roll on the ground, leap, fall, clutch the bottle and fling it away, all with such abandon and fury that it had Louis flinching.

There was a comic interlude to follow: a fool-faced vendor of eggs strolled through the audience and tried to sell them, a clown-faced policeman accosted him with a rubber truncheon and dragged him off to a frowning judge with a cotton-wool beard who made a fool of himself by asking the vendor totally absurd and irrelevant questions till the egg vendor, exasperated, seized the policeman's truncheon and brought it down on the judge's head. The crowd roared. Louis felt he should now edge away and disappear. There was no need to be an onlooker at a market sideshow along with vegetable sellers and tortilla eaters.

But the dancer had returned to the ring and Louis, looking back, saw his feline body stalk across the space with the kind of authority that rivets an onlooker. Besides, Louis caught sight of another figure strutting across the ring from the other direction, towards him and past him – a girl in blue jeans and a white T-shirt, ordinary laced black shoes, her hair cut short to her shoulders, no make-up or costume, but with a dancer's controlled grace and carefully considered movements that invested the faintest turn of her head or twist of the wrist with significance. Louis was held by that grace and authority, and as he stared it dawned on him who she was: Arturo's kid sister, one of the two little girls who had smiled at him when he visited, sometimes played basketball in the garden with the boys, and for whom he had developed boyishly sentimental feelings he never confessed to anyone, scarcely even to himself. Ester and Isabel – he remembered their names now: which one was she? He glanced across at Arturo who was standing at the top of the stairs, watching, his arms folded about him, and his expression – watchful, proprietorial, concerned – confirmed his impression: this was Isabel, or perhaps Ester, grown into this astonishing young sylph, dancing with the man in black as he had never seen anyone dance in the city, at clubs or parties. Where had she learned to dance like that – in that man's embrace, or rejected by him and on her own, then with a second dancer who entered the arena and prowled around, waiting for his chance and taking it? Here was Ester – or Isabel – and now she was grown-up, and dancing amongst grown-ups, performing, acting out those rites of attraction, infatuation, rejection and recovery that Louis had not only not experienced yet but not witnessed anyone in his circle of family and friends experience with such ardour, abandon and intensity.

The trio met in the centre of the ring and performed their dance together, then parted, stalking off in different directions, and Alejandro was returning, holding his guitar above his head, when Louis broke away and pushed his way out past the onlookers.

He hurried past the lurid murals, the huarache sellers and the comic-book stalls under the trees by the bandstand and out onto Avenida de Revolution 1910 without thinking. It was the wrong direction, he realised, and he would have to walk down its length before he could take the turn that led him back to Matamoros – Matamoros where Dona Celia kept the old house as it had always been, and the world at bay.

The entire street was jammed with the gaieties of the Sunday market, shoppers strolling in the sun, picking through stalls of silver trinkets, scarves and blouses, paper flowers and painted mirrors. The ice cream and sorbet stall, festooned with pink and blue pompoms, was so busy it was hard to get past it. The middle of the street was taken up by the young, sipping margaritas from clay mugs, or large families enjoying helados. The women wore high heels and low-cut blouses, dark glasses and jewellery, the young girls had tinted hair, painted nails and laughing mouths and young men pressed against them, admiring.

These were the people from Cuernavaca and Mexico City to whose parties Louis went when he was at home; these were the girls with whom he danced, the young men with whom he played tennis. If there were a golf club here, then these were the people who would play on its course. His family would urge him to join them: he belonged, they belonged, to the same society. He did not belong to the people under the marquee – they would have been strangers to his family, and they would have looked upon him as an onlooker, and an outsider.

Then what made him push his way out of their company and stumble through the gate to the convento and seek out its calm, cool cloisters? He had always liked to come here, for its quiet and shade and vast views of the mountains and valleys from its deep windows. It had always been an oasis to which he could withdraw, for contemplation.

> In the court, the sun stone, immobile;
> above, the sun of fire and of time turns;
> movement is sun and the sun is stone.

Now he walked down the shaded veranda under a ceiling painted with crimson roses not quite faded into the stone, and entered the courtyard where water dropped quietly from a fountain set amongst grass paths and potted bougainvillaea. But above it hung a strange, unfamiliar shape fashioned out of wicker and fastened by ropes to the belfry. What was it? He climbed the stairs to the upper galleries for a closer look at the wicker basket – or was it a trap? – and found the galleries hung with art exhibits and remembered that that was the use to which the convento was nowadays put. If this could be called an art exhibit: the exhibition clearly had to do with Tepoztlan's environment – the subject could not be avoided, it confronted him wherever he went. Here were photogaphs of its flowers and birds, here were installations of sand scattered with ugly litter – Coke cans, plastic bolsas – and paintings of devastated landscapes, pitted and marred by modern, urban blight, photographs of the aged, their weathered faces looking out of doorways and windows, watching.

Louis caught his breath. Was there no escape from Tepoztlan's issues and involvements, its demands and accusations? And whose side *was* he on? Everything, everyone he encountered seemed to ask him to decide, to declare.

It was late afternoon when he finally turned into Avenida Matamoros, and early clouds had begun to descend from the mountains. The bamboo grove threw long shadows across the white dust and in it sprawled men he'd seen earlier, heavily asleep. He had to avoid stumbling on their limp figures and empty bottles. He turned in at the gate and shut it quickly behind him.

In the shadowy drawing room Dona Celia was seated stiffly as an idol but on seeing him began at once to complain about how the town had gone to pieces and wanted to know if he had noticed the deterioration. Who, what is it that has deteriorated but you, you old ghost? he wanted to ask and to say that everyone else was moving on, on, but instead he muttered his impressions as noncomittally as possible. Nadyn, who was poking at a Raidolito with a hairpin and blinking against its fumes, interrupted to ask if he had met any of his old friends. What were they doing now? she wanted to know as if confident he would reply 'Nothing' at which she could pull a face, but he turned it into 'I don't know', disappointing her.

'There's nothing to know. The young today – pah!' snorted Dona Celia, drawing her shawl about her throat with a malevolent glare.

It was a relief when Teresa announced dinner and they rose to go and sit at a table where she had placed a pot of pozole and stood waiting for Louis to take his first spoonful. 'Good?' she queried. 'As good as before, eh?'

Nadyn looked up and frowned at her but Dona Celia herself was giving the soup her approval, slurping it up with indiscreet sounds that expressed relish – in spite of everything, expressed relish.

Louis had to wait till Teresa was gone before saying to his aunt, 'I will be leaving in the morning. Please don't let me disturb you – so early – I'll let myself out –'

What? Dona Celia's expression managed to say, after another quick, delicious swallow. Slowly her look of pleasure was overtaken by the habitual displeasure. So soon? He had only just come. 'And are you not staying for Cousin Heriberto's birthday celebration? It is to be a very big celebration, you know. He is eighty years old this week.' All his children were coming, from Monterey, from Toluca – even Louis' parents had spoken of coming. Why then –

His thesis. His classes. The university – But not in the summer, surely? Research had to be continued, you see, no rest for the weary. He flushed as he stumbled over his excuses and Nadyn watched with a tightening of her lips – she of course saw through them instantly. Her pride at never having made them herself gave her mouth a bitter twist.

'We're too old for you, not up to date, eh?' she said. 'Ah, the gringo –'

He wanted to protest but the words disintegrated in his mouth, useless. He lowered his eyes to the bowl of soup, Teresa's excellent pozole. He felt ashamed of not doing it the honour it deserved.

The Rooftop Dwellers

PAYING off the autorickshaw driver, she stepped down cautiously, clutching her handbag to her. The colony was much further out than she had expected – they had travelled through bazaars and commerical centres and suburbs she had not known existed – but the name given on the gate matched the one in her purse. She went up to it and rattled the latch to announce her arrival. Immediately a dog began to yap and she could tell by its shrillness that it was one of those small dogs that readily sink their tiny teeth into one's ankle or rip through the edge of one's sari. There were also screams from several children. Yet no one came to open the gate for her and finally she let herself in, hoping the dog was chained or indoors. Certainly there was no one in the tiny garden which consisted of a patch of lawn and a tap in front of the yellow stucco villa. All the commotion appeared to be going on indoors and she walked up to the front door – actually at the side of the house – and rang the bell, clearing her throat like a saleswoman preparing to sell a line in knitting patterns or home-made jams.

She was finally admitted by a very small servant boy in striped cotton pyjamas and a torn grey vest, and taken to meet the family. They were seated on a large bed in the centre of a room with walls painted an electric blue, all watching a show on a gigantic television set. It was an extremely loud, extremely dramatic scene showing a confrontation between a ranting hero, a weeping heroine and a benignly smiling saint, and the whole family was watching open-mouthed, reluctant to turn their attention away from it. But when their dog darted out from under the bed at her, she screamed and the servant boy flapped his duster and cried, 'No, Candy! Get down, Candy!' they had no alternative but to turn to her, resentfully.

'You have come just at *Mahabharata* time,' the woman crosslegged on the bed reproached her.

'Sit down, sit down, beti. You can watch it with us,' the man said more agreeably, waving at an open corner on the bed, and since they had all transferred their attention back to the screen, she was forced to perch on it, fearfully holding her ankles up in the air so as not to be nipped by Candy, who had been driven back under the bed and hid there, growling. The two children stared at her for a bit, impassively, then went back to picking their noses and following the episode of the *Mahabharata* that the whole city of Delhi watched, along with the rest of the country, on Sunday evenings – everyone, except for her.

There had been too much happening in her life to leave room for watching television and keeping up with the soap operas and mythological sagas. In any case, there was no television set in the women's hostel where she had a room. There was nothing in it except what was absolutely essential: the dining room on the ground floor with its long tables, its benches, its metal plates and utensils, and the kitchen with its hatch through which the food appeared in metal pots; and upstairs the rows of rooms, eight feet by ten, each equipped with a wooden bedframe, and a shelf nailed to the wall. She had had to purchase a plastic bucket to take to the bathroom at the end of the corridor so she could bathe under the standing tap — not high enough to work as a shower — and had arranged her toilet articles on the shelf and left her clothes in her tin trunk which she covered with a pink tablecloth and sat on when she did not want to sit on her bed, or when one of the other women in the hostel came to visit her and climbed onto her bed to have a chat.

The minimalism of these living arrangements was both a novelty and a shock to her. She came from a home where the accommodation of objects, their comfortable clutter and convenience, could be taken for granted. Nothing had been expensive or elaborate but there had been plenty of whatever there was, accumulated over many years: rugs, chairs, cushions, clothes, dishes, in rooms, verandas, odd corners and spaces. So for the first two weeks she felt she was trapped in a cell; whenever she shut the door, she was swallowed by the cell, its prisoner. If she left the door ajar, every girl going past would look in, scream, 'Oh, Moy-na!' and come in to talk, tell her of the latest atrocity committed by the matron or of the unbelievably rotten food being served downstairs, and also of their jobs, their bosses, their colleagues, and homes and families. Some were divorcees, some widows, and some supported large families, all of which led to an endless fund of stories to be told. In order to get any sleep, she would have to shut the door and pretend not to be in. Then she began to wonder if she was in herself.

But such was her determination to make her new life as a working woman in the metropolis succeed, and such was her unexpected, unforeseen capacity for adjustment, that after a month or so the minimalism became no longer privation and a challenge but simply a way of life. She even found herself stopping at her neighbours' open doors on her way back from the office, to say, 'D'you know what they're cooking for our dinner downstairs?' and laughing when the others groaned, invariably, 'Pumpkin!' because that was all there ever was, or else to give the warning, 'Matron's *mad*! I heard her screaming at Leila — she found out about her iron. Hide yours, quick!' It became a habit, instead of a subject of complaint, to carry her bucket down to the bathroom when she wanted to bathe, and bring it back to her room so it wouldn't be stolen: thefts were common, unfortunately. Even the tap, and water, began to seem like luxuries, bonuses not to be taken for granted in that hostel.

After a breakfast of tea, bread and fried eggs, she went out to stand at the bus stop with the other women, all of whom caught the Ladies' Special that came around at nine o'clock and carried them to their work places as telephone operators, typists, desk receptionists, nurses, teachers, airline hostesses and bank tellers, without the menace of crazed young men groping at them or pressing into them as if magnetised, or even delivering vicious pinches before leaping off the bus and running for their lives. Some women had had to develop defensive strategies. Lily, known to be 'bold', instructed others to carry a sharp pin concealed in their fists and use that to prod anyone who came too close. 'I've made big men cry,' she boasted proudly, but most women in the hostel preferred to pay the extra rupee or two to travel on the Ladies' Special instead of the regular DTS. Like tap water, it was a luxury, a bonus, which had their gratitude.

Moyna's descriptions of these strategies of living earned her the admiration of her family and friends back at home to whom she described them, but trouble began for her just as she was settling into this new, challenging way of life. She came across the hostel cook kicking viciously at the skeletal yellow kitten that had crept in from outside in the hope of one of life's unexpected bonuses – a drop of milk left in someone's tumbler, or a scrap from the garbage bin. Instinctively she lowered her hand and called it to her – she came from a home that was shelter to an assortment of cats, dogs, birds, some maimed, some pregnant, some dying. She shared her bread and fried egg with the kitten, and soon it started weaving in and out of her sari folds, then followed her up the stairs and darted into her room. This was novelty indeed: having someone to share the cell with her. It was curious how instantly the room ceased to be a prison. The kitten settled onto the pink tablecloth on the trunk and began to lick itself clean, delicately raising one leg at a time into the air and making a thorough toilet, as if it were preparing to be fit for such luxurious accommodation. Later, that night, she woke to find it had sprung from the trunk to her bed. Knowing it probably had fleas, she tried to kick it off, but it clung on and started to purr, as if to persuade her of its accomplishments. Purring, it lay against her leg and lulled her back to sleep.

One day the matron was inspecting during the day, when they were all away, for such forbidden items as irons and hot plates, and came out holding the kitten by the scruff of his neck. Moyna pleaded innocence and swore she did not know how he had got into her room. But when she was caught red-handed, emptying the milk jug into a saucer for Mao under the table, the matron slapped her with the eviction notice. Had Moyna not read the rule: No Pets Allowed?

Instinctively, she knew not to mention Mao to this family. Somehow that would have to be sorted out, if she took the room they had to offer. But, glancing round at their faces in the flickering light from the television set, she began to feel uncertain if she would take it. At her office, Tara, who was experienced in these matters, had told her, 'You don't have to take the first room you see, Moyna. You can look around and *choose*.' But Moyna had already 'looked around' and while, by comparison with the cell in the women's hostel, all the rooms had seemed princely, shamingly it was she who had been turned down by one prospective landlord or landlady after the other. She had been scrutinised with such suspicion, questioned with such hostility, that she realised that no matter what they stated in their advertisements, they had nothing but fear and loathing for the single working woman, and the greatest dread of allowing one into their safe, decent homes. Moyna wondered how she could convey such an impression of sin and wantonness. She dressed in a clean, starched cotton sari every day, and even though her hair was cut short, it was simply pinned back behind her ears, not curled or dyed. And surely her job in the office of a literary journal was innocent enough? But they narrowed their eyes, saw her as too young, too pretty, too unattached, too much an *instrument* of danger, and dismissed her as a candidate for their barsatis. These rooms had once been built on Delhi's flat rooftops so that families who slept out on their roofs on summer nights could draw in their beds in case of a sudden dust storm or thunder shower. But now that Delhi was far too unsafe for sleeping alfresco, these barsatis were being rented out to working spinsters or bachelors at a delightful profit.

Suddenly convinced that she would not, after all, want to occupy this unwelcoming family's barsati, Moyna lowered her feet to the floor gingerly and tried to rise and murmur an excuse. 'I have to be at the hostel before nine,' she said when the episode of the *Mahabharata* ended with a great display of fiery arrows being shot into the sky and a whirling disc beheading the villain. The landlord gestured to the children to turn off the set and, turning to Moyna, he shouted to the servant boy to bring her a drink. 'What will you have, beti? Chai, lassi, lemonade?'

'No, thank you, no, thank you,' she murmured, seeing the landlady's steely eyes on her, willing her to refuse, but the servant boy came out with a thick glass of tepid water for her anyway. While she sipped it, the inquisition began, interrupted frequently by the children who alternately demanded their dinner or another show on television and by the dog who emerged from under the bed and sniffed at her suspiciously. Moyna kept her eyes lowered to watch for Candy and perhaps they saw that as becoming modesty or demureness because, to her surprise, the landlady said, 'You want to see the room? Ramu, Ramu – eh, Ramu! Get the key to the barsati and open it up.'

And there, on the flat rooftop of the plain yellow stucco villa in a colony Moyna had never heard of before on the outskirts of New Delhi, there to her astonishment was a palace, a veritable palace amongst barsatis. The rooftop, which covered the entire area of the villa, seemed to her immense, larger than any space she had occupied since her arrival in Delhi, and it was clear, empty space under an empty sky, with a view of all the other rooftops stretching out on every side, giving Moyna, as she stood there, a sense of being the empress of all she surveyed. Of course it would bake under her feet in the heat of summer but – and this was the crowning glory – a pipal tree that grew in the small walled courtyard at the back of the house rose up over the barsati itself, sheltering it from the sun with a canopy of silvery, rustling leaves, spreading out its branches and murmuring, Moyna felt certain, a gracious welcome.

After that auspicious view, what could it matter if the barsati itself was merely a square walled cube, that it had not been cleaned in so long that its single window had turned opaque with dust, and spider-webs hung in swags from every corner, that the bed was nothing but a string cot, the cheapest kind of charpai? What did it matter that the single cupboard against the wall had doors that did not seem to meet but sagged on their hinges and could never be locked, that the 'kitchen' was only a blackened kerosene stove atop a wooden table that also served as desk and dining table, that the 'bathroom' was a closet-sized attached enclosure, open to the sky, with a very stained and yellowed squatter-type toilet and a single stand-pipe? Already Moyna's mind was racing with visions of what she could transform the place into. Why, its very bareness gave her the freedom to indulge her wildest dreams and fancies.

Then her look fell upon the servant boy who stood waiting by the door that opened onto the staircase, twirling the key round his finger and smirking, and she became aware that she herself had a smile across her face and that her hands were clasped to her throat in a most foolish fashion. Immediately she dropped them, adjusted her expression to one of severity, and followed him down the stairs.

The landlord and landlady, now risen from the bed and waiting for her on the veranda, looking as alike as twins with their corpulence, their drooping chins and expressions of benign self-satisfaction, appeared confident of her answer: it was only what could be expected after seeing what they were offering. She would of course sign a year's lease which could be terminated whenever they chose, pay three months' deposit, plus the first month's rent right now, immediately, 'and we will welcome you to our house as our own beti,' they assured her magnanimously. 'From now on, you need worry about nothing. Your parents need have no worries about you. We will be your parents.'

Tara came over from the office with her husband Ritwick to help her to move in. Moyna had only one tin trunk, a bedding roll and now her kitten in a basket, but they insisted she would not be able to move on her own, and Ritwick growled that he wanted to meet the Bhallas 'to make sure'. The Bhallas were seated on a wicker sofa in the veranda when they arrived, and watched them carry every item up the stairs with openly inquisitve stares. It seemed to Moyna that it was not Ritwick who was sizing them up so much as that they were sizing *him* up. Certainly they questioned him closely, when Moyna introduced him to them, regarding his parentage, ancestral home, present occupation and relation to Tara and Moyna before allowing him to set one foot on the stairs. But once they arrived on the rooftop, Ritwick looked into every crack and crevice with a suspicion to equal theirs. Then he asked, 'Where's the water tank?'

'What water tank?'

'*Your* water tank. Where is your water supply coming from?'

'I don't know. Where *does* it come from? The pipes, I suppose.'

He strode to the bathroom and turned on the tap. It spun around weakly, gurgled in a complaining tone, and sputtered into silence. There was no water. Moyna stood in the doorway, stricken. 'Water shortage,' she explained. 'You know Delhi has a water shortage, Ritwick.'

'Not if you have a storage tank. Everyone has a storage tank – or several. The Bhallas will have one downstairs, but you need a booster pump and your own tank up here so water can be pumped up from the one below.'

'Oh.'

He looked at her with the kind of exasperation her own brothers turned on her when she failed to understand what they were doing under the bonnet of the car or with electric gadgets at home. She came from a family so competent that she had never needed to be competent herself.

'Did you ask the Bhallas about it?'

'About what?'

'The storage tank. The booster pump.'

'No,' she admitted.

He strode off towards the staircase with every show of determination to enquire immediately. She ran after him, crying, 'Oh, Ritwick, I'll ask them – I'll ask them – later, when I go down.'

Tara came out of the barsati. 'D'you have curtains?'

'What for?'

'Because if you wipe the windowpanes clean, your neighbours can look right in.'

'No, they can't! There's the tree – don't you see my beautiful tree? It's like a screen.'

'Come in and see.'

Tara had wiped the windowpanes clean, and a young man with a face like a pat of butter and with a small moustache twitching over his pursed lips was standing on his rooftop and gazing at them with unconcealed curiosity and, it could easily be made out since the distance was small, some admiration.

'Oh, Tara, why did you go and clean that?' Moyna cried. 'No, I don't have a curtain. Where would I get a curtain from?'

'Get me a bedsheet then,' Tara commanded, 'and help me put it up at once.'

'But the tree –' Moyna tried again, and went out to see why it had not lowered a branch where it was needed. The tree shaded the entire barsati (and Ritwick admitted it would keep off the sun which would otherwise make a tandoori oven of it) but it was tall and provided no screen against the other rooftops and the rooftop dwellers who suddenly all seemed to be standing outside their barsati doors, surveying this newcomer to their level of elevation. Moyna suddenly realised she had joined a community.

'When I came yesterday, I saw no one,' she mumbled, abashed.

'Well, you can introduce yourself to all of them now,' Ritwick said, 'and just hope none of them are thieves or murderers because if they are –' he looked grim and gestured – 'all they need is one jump from their ledge to yours.'

'Don't, Ritwick,' Tara said sharply. 'Why are you trying to frighten poor Moyna?'

'All I'm saying is Moyna'd better stay indoors and keep her door locked.'

'But I was going to drag my bed out and sleep under the stars!'

'Are you *crazy*?' both Tara and Ritwick said together, and

Tara added, 'D'you want your picture in the evening news, with a headline: "Single Woman robbed and murdered in barsati"?' They looked at her sternly to see if their words had had the requisite effect, and Tara added, 'Now let's go to the market and get you all the things you need. Like one great big lock and key.'

When they returned from the market with cleaning fluids, brooms, scrubbing materials, provisions for 'the kitchen' – and the lock and key – Ritwick confronted the landlady who had in the meantime shampooed her hair and now sat on the veranda, to dry it in the sun.

'Excuse me,' he said, not very politely. 'Can you please show Moyna where the switch is for the booster pump?'

'What switch? What booster pump?' She parted her hair and peered out from under it with some hostility.

'Is there no booster pump to send water up to the barsati?'

'Water up to the barsati?' she repeated, as if he were mad. 'Why? Why? What is wrong?'

'There's no water in the tap. She'll need water, won't she?'

'She will get water,' declared Mrs Bhalla, drawing herself up and tossing her head so that the grey strands flew, 'when municipality is sending water. Municipality water is coming at five o'clock every morning and five o'clock every evening. The barsati will be getting water whenever municipality sends.'

'At five in the morning and five in the evening?' shouted Ritwick. 'You need a storage tank so water will collect.'

'Collect? Why she cannot collect in a bucket?' Mrs Bhalla shouted back. 'She has no bucket?' she added insultingly.

Tara and Moyna were standing with their purchases in their arms, ready to bolt upstairs, but Ritwick yelled, 'Yes, she *has* bucket, but how can she collect at five in the morning and five in the evening?'

'What is wrong?' Mrs Bhalla screamed back. 'We are all collecting – why she cannot collect also?'

'Because she will be sleeping at five in the morning and at work at five in the evening!'

Mrs Bhalla turned away from him and looked at her tenant with an expression that made clear what she thought of any young woman who would be asleep at five in the morning and 'at work' at five in the evening. She clearly had an equally low opinion of sleep and work, at least where her young tenant was concerned. Ritwick was shouting, 'Storage tank – booster pump –' when Moyna fled upstairs, dropping matchboxes and kitchen dusters along the way. When Tara followed her up, she found her sitting on her bed in tears, howling, 'And I've signed the lease for one year and paid for three months in advance!'

Moyna's way of life changed completely. It had to be adjusted to that of the Bhallas. She left her tap turned on when she went to bed – which she did earlier and earlier – so she could be woken by the sound of water gushing into the plastic bucket at five in the morning and get up to fill every pot, pan and kettle she had acquired before turning it off. All around her she could hear her fellow rooftop dwellers performing the same exercise – as well as bathing and washing clothes in the starlight before the water ran out. She went back to bed and lay there, panting, trying to get back to sleep, but by six o'clock all the birds that roosted in the pipal tree were awake and screaming and running on their little clawed feet across the corrugated iron roof, then lining up along the ledge of the rooftop to flutter their wings, crow, squawk and chirp their ode to dawn. It was just as well that they made it impossible for her to fall asleep again because at six she had to go downstairs and walk to the market where Mother Dairy would have opened its booth and all the colony residents would be lining up with their milk cans to have them filled. She stood there with all the servant boys and maidservants, sleepy-eyed, for the the sake of having her milk pail filled for Mao, and then carried it back carefully through the dust, in her slippers, trying not to spill any.

No Ladies' Special serviced this colony, and Tara had warned her against attempting to travel to work on an ordinary DTS bus. 'You don't know what men in Delhi do to women,' she said darkly. 'This isn't Bombay or Calcutta, you know.'

Moyna had heard this warning in the women's hostel but asked, 'What d'you mean?'

'In Calcutta all men call women Mother or Sister and never touch them. In Bombay, if any man did, the woman would give him a tight slap and drag him by his hair to the police station. But in Delhi – these Jats . . .', she shuddered, adding, 'Don't you even *try*.'

So Moyna walked back to the marketplace after breakfast, to the autorickshaw stand in front of Mother Dairy, and spent a sizeable part of her income on taking one to work. She clearly made a woebegone figure while waiting, and a kindly Sikh who rode his autorickshaw as if it were a sturdy ox, his slippered feet planted on either side of the gearbox, the end of his turban flying, and a garland of tinsel twinkling over the dashboard where he had pasted a photograph of his two children and an oleograph of Guru Gobind Singh, took pity on her. 'Beti, every day you go to work at the same time, to the same place. I will take you, for a monthly rate. It will be cheaper for you.' So Gurmail Singh became her private chauffeur, so to speak, and Moyna rode to work bouncing on the narrow backseat, her sari held over her nose to keep out the dust and oil and diesel fumes from all the office-bound traffic through which he expertly threaded his way. Quite often he was waiting for her outside the office at six o'clock to take her home. 'I live in that colony myself, so it is no trouble to me,' he told her. 'If I have no other customer, I can take you, why not?' In a short while she got to know his entire family – his mother who cooked the best dhal in the land, and the finest corn bread and mustard greens, his daughter who was the smartest student in her class – class two, he told Moyna – and his son who had only just started going to school but was unfortunately not showing the same keen interest in his studies as his sister. 'I tell him, "Do you want to go back to the village and herd buffaloes?" But he doesn't care, his heart is only in play. When it is school-time, he cries. And his mother cries with him.'

'Gurmail Singh thinks it is the school that is bad. Bluebells, it's called,' Moyna reported at the office. 'He wants to get him into a good convent school, like St Mary's, but you need pull for that.' She sighed, lacking any.

'Moyna, can't you talk about anything but the Bhallas and Gurmail Singh and his family?' Tara asked one day, stubbing out her cigarette in an ashtray on her desk.

Moyna was startled: she had not realised she was growing so obsessive about these people, so prominent in her life, so uninteresting to her colleagues. But didn't Tara talk about Ritwick's position in the university, and about her own son and his trials at school, or the hardships of having to live with her widowed mother-in-law for lack of their own house? 'What d'you want to talk about then?' she asked, a little hurt.

'Look, we have to bring out the magazine, don't we?' Tara said, smoking furiously. 'And it isn't getting easier, it just gets harder all the time to get people to read a journal about *books*. Bose Sahib hardly comes to see what is going on here –' she complained.

'What is going on?' asked Raj Kumar, the peon, bringing them two mugs of coffee from the shop downstairs. 'I am here, running everything for you. Why do you need Bose Sahib?'

'Oh, Raj Kumar,' Tara sighed, putting out her cigarette and accepting the rich, frothing coffee from him. 'What will you do to make *Books* sell?'

Tara was the first person Ajoy Bose had employed when he started his literary review, *Books*, after coming to Delhi as a member of parliament from Calcutta. He had missed the literary life of that city so acutely, and had been so appalled by the absence of any equivalent in New Delhi, that he had decided to publish a small journal of book reviews to inform readers on what was being published, what might be read, a service no other magazine seemed to provide, obsessed as they all were with politics or the cinema, the only two subjects that appeared to bring people in the capital to life. Having first met Ritwick at the Jawaharlal Nehru University during a conference on Karl Marx and Twentieth Century Bengali Literature, and through him Tara, he had engaged her as the Managing Editor. The office was installed in two rooms above a coffee and sweet shop in Bengali Market. It was Tara's first paid job – she had been working in non-government organisations simply to escape from home and her mother-in-law – and she was extremely proud of these two modest rooms that she had furnished with cane mats and bamboo screens. Bose Sahib had magnanimously installed a desert cooler and a water cooler to keep life bearable in the summer heat. Together they had interviewed Raj Kumar, and found him literate enough to run their errands at the post office and bank. Then Tara had interviewed all the candidates who had applied for the post of assistant, and chosen Moyna. Moyna had no work experience at all, having only just taken her degree, in English literature, at a provincial university. She managed somehow to convey her need to escape from family and home, and Tara felt both maternal and proprietorial towards her, while Moyna immensely admired her style, the way she smoked cigarettes and drank her coffee black and spoke to both Raj Kumar and Bose Sahib as equals, and she hoped ardently to emulate her, one day.

Of course the only reason she had been allowed by her family to come to Delhi and take the job was that it was of a literary nature, and her father had known Bose Sahib at the university. They approved of all she told them in her weekly letters and, Moyna often thought while opening parcels of books that had arrived from the publishers or upon receiving stacks of printed copies of their journal fresh from the press, how proud they would be if they could see her, their youngest, and how incredulous . . .

Now here was Tara claiming that sales were so poor as to be shameful, and that if no one came to its rescue, the journal would fold. 'Just look at our list of subscribers,' Tara said disgustedly, tossing it over the desk to Moyna. 'It's the same list Bose Sahib drew up when we began — we haven't added one new subscriber in the last year!'

'Oh, Tara, my father is now a subscriber,' Moyna reminded her nervously, but Tara glared at her so she felt compelled to study the list seriously. It was actually quite interesting: apart from the names of a few of Bose Sahib's fellow members of parliament, and a scattering of college libraries, the rest of the list was made up of a circle so far-flung as to read like a list of the rural districts of India. She could not restrain a certain admiration. 'Srimati Shakuntala Pradhan in PO Barmana, Dist. Bilaspur, HP, and Sri Rajat Khanna in Dist. Birbhum, 24 Parganas, W. Bengal . . . Tara, just think of all the places the journal *does* get to! We ought to have a map on the wall –'

Raj Kumar, who was listening while washing out the coffee mugs in the corner with the water cooler which stood in a perennial puddle, called out heartily, 'Yes, and I am posting it from Gole Market Post Office to the whole of Bharat! Without me, no one is getting *Books*!'

Moyna turned to throw him a look of mutual congratulation but Tara said, 'Shut up, Raj Kumar. If we can't find new names for our list, we'll lose the special rate the post office gives journals.'

'Send to bogus names, then, and bogus addresses!' Raj Kumar returned smartly.

Now Tara turned to stare at him. 'How do you know so much about such bogus tricks?'

He did not quite give her a wink but, as he polished the mugs with a filthy rag, he began to hum the latest hit tune from the Bombay cinema which was the great love of his life and the bane of the two women's.

'The next time Bose Sahib comes, we'll really have to have a serious discussion,' Tara said. The truth was that her son Bunty had received such a bad report from school that it was clear he would need tutoring in maths as well as Hindi, and that would mean paying two private tutors on top of the school fees which were by no means negligible – and the matter of Ritwick's promotion had still not been brought up for consideration. She lit another cigarette nervously.

Bose only came to visit them when parliament opened for its summer session. He, too, had much on his mind – in his case, of a political nature – and *Books* was not a priority for him. But when he was met on the appointed day at the door by two such anxious young women, and saw the coffee and the Gluco biscuits spread out on Tara's desk in preparation for his announced visit, he realised this was not to be a casual visit but a business conference. He cleared his throat and sat down to listen to their problems with all the air of an MP faced with his constituents.

'So, we have to have a sales drive, eh?' he said after listening to Tara spell out the present precarious state of the journal.

'Yes, but before we have that, we have to have an overhaul,' Tara told him authoritatively. 'For instance, Bose Sahib, the name *Books* just has to go. I told you straightaway it is the most boring, unattractive name you could think up –'

'What do you mean? What do you mean?' he spluttered, tobacco flakes spilling from his fingers as he tamped them into his pipe. 'What can be more *attractive* than *Books*? What can be less *boring* than *Books*?' He seemed appalled by her philistinism.

'Oh, that's just for *you*.' Tara was not in the least put out by the accusation in his mild face or his eyes blinking behind the thick glasses in their black frames. 'What about people browsing in a shop, seeing all these magazines with pin-ups and headlines? Are they going to *glance* at a journal with a plain yellow cover like a school note book, with just the word *Books* on it?'

'Why not? Why not?' he spluttered, still agitated.

'Perhaps we could choose a new title?' Moyna suggested, rubbing her fingers along the scratches on the desk, nervously.

The two women had already discussed the matter between them, and now spilled out their suggestions: *The Book Bag, The Book Shelf* . . . well, perhaps those weren't so much more exciting than plain *Books* but what about, what about — *Pen and Ink? The Pen Nib? Pen and Paper? Press and Paper?*

It seemed to make Bose Sahib think that new blood was required on the staff because his reaction to their session was to send them, a month later, a new employee he had taken on, a young man newly graduated from the University of Hoshiarpur who would aid Tara and Moyna in all their office chores. He would deal with the press, see the paper through the press, supervise its distribution, visit bookshops and persuade them to display the journal more prominently, and allow Tara and Moyna to take on extra work such as hunting for new subscribers and advertisers.

Tara and Moyna were not at all sure if they liked the new arrangement or if they really wanted anyone else on the staff. As for Raj Kumar, he was absolutely sure he did not. No warm reception had been planned for the graduate from Hoshiarpur University (in the opinion of Tara and Moyna, there could be no instituition of learning on a lower rung of the ladder) but when young Mohan appeared, they had been disarmed. By his woebegone looks and low voice they learned he no more wanted to be there than they wanted to have him there, that he had merely been talked into it by his professor, an old friend of Bose Sahib's. He himself was very sad to leave Hoshiarpur where his mother and four sisters provided him with a life of comfort. The very thought of those comforts made his eyes dewy when he told Tara and Moyna of the food he ate at home, the grilled chops, the egg curries, the biryanis and home-made pickles. Moreover, if it was necessary to begin a life of labour so young — he had only graduated three months ago and hardly felt prepared for the working life — then he had hoped for something else.

'What *would* you have liked to do, Mohan?' Moyna asked him sympathetically (she was not at all certain if she was cut out for a career at *Books* either).

'Travel and Tourism,' he announced without hesitation. 'One friend of mine, he is in Travel and Tourism and he is having a fine time — going to airport, receiving foreign tourists, taking them to five-star hotels in rented cars, with chauffeurs — and receiving tips. Fine time he is having, and much money also, in tips.'

Moyna felt so sorry for the sad contrast provided by *Books* that she asked Raj Kumar to fetch some samosas for them to have with their tea. Mohan slurped his up from a saucer, and when Raj Kumar returned with the samosas in an oily newspaper packet, he snapped up two without hesitation. Moyna wondered if he was living in a barsati: she thought she saw signs that he did. Wiping his fingers on Raj Kumar's all-purpose duster, Mohan remarked, 'Not so good as my sister makes.'

Tara thought Moyna could go out in search of advertisements, but when Moyna looked terror-struck and helpless, and cried, 'Oh, but I don't even know Delhi, Tara,' she got up, saying resignedly, 'All right, we'll do the rounds together, just this once,' and gave Raj Kumar and Mohan a string of instructions before leaving the office. Putting on her dark glasses, slinging her handbag over her shoulder, and hailing an autorickshaw that was idling outside the coffee shop, Tara looked distinctly cheerful at the prospect.

Moyna could not see what there was to be cheerful about: the publishing houses they visited were all in the back lanes of Darya Ganj and Kashmere Gate, far from salubrious to her way of thinking, particularly on a steaming afternoon in late summer, and the publishers they met all seemed oppressed by the weather, slumped in their offices listlessly, under slowly revolving fans – if the electricity had not broken down altogether, in which case they would be plunged in gloom, in dim candlelight – and they seemed far from interested in increasing sales of their wares by advertising in *Books*. 'We have been advertising,' one reminded them brusquely, 'for more than two years, and we are seeing no increase in sales. Who is reading *Books*? Nobody is reading.' Tara looked extremely offended and swept out with great dignity after reminding him that he had yet to pay for the advertisements he had placed. Moyna followed her, quietly impressed if uncertain as to whether she could bring off a confrontation so satisfactorily.

They had a little better luck with the bookshops in Connaught Place and Khan Market which were not nearly so depressing and were often run by pleasant proprietors who sent out for Campa Cola and Fanta for them, and at times even agreed to place a few advertisements of their best-selling thrillers. The bookshop for the publications of the USSR – mostly cheerful and cheap translations of Russian folk tales and fables in bright colours for children – proved particularly supportive. A charming Russian gentleman gave them a free calendar and a brochure listing the film, dance and music programmes at Tolstoy Bhavan. Encouraged, Tara suggested they visit the British Council next. 'But do they publish books?' Moyna asked. She was dusty, hot and very tired by now. Tara thought that irrelevant – they could advertise their library, couldn't they?

Actually, they could not, and did not, but the young man they spoke to, who had been summoned out of his office to deal with them, was so apologetic about the refusal that they gave him a copy of the latest edition of *Books* gratis. He looked overcome, pushing back a lock of his fair hair from his forehead and gazing at the magazine as if it were a work of art. 'Oh,' he said, several times, 'how perfectly splendid. Perfectly splendid, really.' Tara straightened her shoulders and gave Moyna a significant look before rising to her feet and making her departure. Moyna followed her reluctantly: the lobby of the British Council library had the best air-conditioning they had run into all day. After that – and the discreet lighting, the carpeting, the soft rustle of newspapers, the attractive look of detective novels and romantic fiction on the shelves – they returned to their office in Bengali Market with a sense of resignation. They did not really expect any results.

But there was Tara at the top of the stairs to the rooftop, pounding on the door and shouting, 'Moyna! Moyna, open up, Moyna!'

Moyna had just been preparing for a bath. It was not entirely uncommon for Tara and Ritwick to drop in on her unannounced if they had managed to persuade Ritwick's mother to mind their little son for a bit, and since she had still not managed to get a telephone installed, there was no way they could warn her. 'Wait a minute,' she called, and slipped back into her clothes before going barefoot across the roof to open the door to them.

Tara was standing there, laughing and in great spirits, not with Ritwick at all but, to Moyna's unconcealed astonishment,

with the fair young man from the British Council, who stood a
few steps lower down, looking more embarrassed even than
before, and clutching in his hands a bottle filled with some
dark liquid. Moyna stared.

'Oh, open the door, Moyna, and let us in. I know you don't
have a phone so how could I warn you? Adrian rang me up
about an advertisement and I asked him to come over, but you
know how the Dragon Lady is in such a temper with me these
days, so I brought him here instead.'

'Oh,' said Moyna doubtfully, thinking of her own Dragon
Lady downstairs.

'*Won't* you let us in?'

Moyna stood aside and then led them towards her barsati.
She really could not have company in there – Tara ought to
know that. Feeling both vexed and embarrassed, she stood in
front of the door now, frowning, and finally said, 'I'll bring
out some chairs,' and left them waiting again. To her
annoyance, Adrian followed her in to help pull out some
chairs, first placing the bottle on the table and saying, 'I
brought you some – um – wine. I thought – um – we could
have a drink together. Um.'

'And I told him you would at least have peanuts –' Tara
shouted from outside.

What could she mean – peanuts? What peanuts? Moyna
frowned. After the chairs, there was the bother with glasses.
What made Tara think she might have wine glasses? All she
could find were two tumblers and a mug – and certainly there
were no peanuts. In fact, she had just finished the last bit of
bread with her dinner, there was not so much as a piece of
toast to offer. But once they were seated on the rooftop, with
the wine poured out, and had had a sip of that, Moyna looked
up to see that the sky still had a pink flush to it, that it was not

entirely dark, that the first stars were beginning to emerge from the day's dust and grime and glare, that the pipal tree was beginning to rustle like a shower of rain in the first breath of air that evening, and suddenly she felt her spirits break free and lift. Here she was, entertaining friends on 'her terrace' on a starry evening, just as she had imagined an adult working woman in the metropolis might do, just as she had imagined *she* would do – and now it was happening. She looked at Adrian, his six narrow feet of height somehow folded onto a small upright chair, and said with incredulity, 'This is nice!' He thought she meant the wine and hurried to refill her glass, blinking happily behind his spectacles.

It was not only she who thought it was nice. Tara seemed liberated by coming away from her mother-in-law's house where she had to live because of Ritwick's stalled promotion at the university. Adrian seemed enchanted by everything his eye encountered on the rooftop – the parrots streaking in to settle in the branches of the pipal tree for the night, the neighbourliness of the other roof dwellers, several of whom had lined up along their ledges to watch (discreetly or not so discreetly) Moyna's first social gathering. Mao the cat jumped upon Adrian's knee and sat there as if on a tall perch with his eyes narrowed to slits, and by the time the bottle of wine was emptied, they had begun to talk much more loudly and laugh more than they were aware. Tara had an endless fund of mother-in-law stories, as Moyna already knew, but Adrian was gratifyingly astounded by them. When Tara told them of the first time Ritwick had brought her to meet his mother and how the first thing she said to Tara was, 'Aré, why are you wearing this pale colour? It does not suit you at all, it makes your complexion muddy,' or of how she would insist Tara wear her wedding jewellery to work 'otherwise people will think you are a widow', Adrian became wide-eyed and gulped, 'She *said* that? You mean she has licence to say what she *likes* to you?' Tara, greatly encouraged, began to exaggerate – as Moyna could tell – and her stories grew wilder and funnier, reducing even Adrian to laughter. The neighbours spied on them, scandalised, hidden now by night's darkness, but they were unaware how their voices carried downstairs as well, and what a degree of grim disapproval was mounting there. When they descended the stairs, Moyna accompanying them with the key to unlock the front gate for them, they found Mr and Mrs Bhalla pacing up and down the small driveway, grey-faced with censure. They had let Candy out from under their bed and now she flew at them, yipping with small snaps of her teeth, till she was curtly called back by Mr Bhalla.

Their looks made Moyna wonder if it was really so late, had they been kept awake? She put on an apologetic look but Tara, on the contrary, threw back her head and said loudly, 'OK, Moyna, good night – see you tomorrow!' and swept out of the gate. Adrian followed her hastily, carefully keeping out of range of Candy's snapping jaws.

Moyna was certain she would have to face the Bhallas' wrath as she turned around, but they drew back and stared at her in silence as she walked up the stairs and vanished.

Although they did not bring it up directly, after that whenever Moyna encountered them, on her way to work or back, they never failed to refer obliquely to that evening. 'You are having more guests tonight?' they would ask when they saw her returning with the shopping she had done along the way. 'No? You seem to be having many friends,' they went on, prodding her to say more. She shook her head, hurrying. 'No? Then why not come and watch TV tonight? *Ramayana* is showing at seven p.m. Very fine film, *Ramayana*. You should join us,' they commanded, as if testing her true colours. She shook her head, making her excuses. 'Oh, then you are going out? With your friends?' they deliberately misunderstood, taunting her. The children, Sweetie and Pinky, giggled behind their fingers.

'Tara, please don't bring Adrian again,' Moyna begged. 'I don't know what my landlord thinks about me. He seems to think I'm some *hostess* or *entertainer*, the way he and his wife go on.'

'Oh, tell them to go to hell,' Tara snapped. 'As if renting their bloody barsati means you can't have any social life.'

'Social life with girls would be all right, but not with *men*, and not with *foreign* men.'

'Really, Moyna,' Tara stared at her and shrugged, 'when are you going to grow up?' Her mother-in-law had clearly had a lot to say about Tara's going out without Ritwick the other evening; Tara showed all the signs of having had a fine row.

'I *am* grown up! I live in a barsati! I don't want to be thrown out of it, that's all.'

Mohan looked up from the omelette he was eating. He had no cooking facilities where he roomed, and the first thing he did on entering the office in the morning was to send Raj Kumar to fetch him a bun omelette which he seemed to greatly enjoy. Wiping up the last streak of grease with the remains of the bun, he said, 'Barsati living is no good for girls. Why not women's hostel?'

She need not have worried about Adrian visiting her again: the look the landlord had given him, plus Candy's warning nips, proved quite enough of a disincentive. The next male to create a problem for Moyna was Mao, now a strapping young tom ready to test his charms in the wider world. No longer willing to stay where she put him, he liked to strut about the barsati roof, or leap up onto the ledge and slowly perform his toilet there where he could be seen, occasionally lifting his head to snarl at a sparrow that mocked and taunted him from a safe distance in the pipal tree, or blink when he became aware of someone watching, possibly admiring him. Moyna feared she would not be able to keep him concealed for long. Already the Bhalla children, Sweetie and Pinky, suspecting his existence, would come up the stairs and peep under the door to catch a glimpse of him, cry, 'Tiger! Tiger!' if they did, and come running pell-mell down the stairs again. They had clearly said something to their mother who would watch Moyna return from the market clutching a wet paper bag reeking of fish and call out, 'Oh, I see you are fond of eating fish!' and had also noted that Moyna took in an unlikely quantity of milk. 'So much milk you are drinking,' she had commented early one morning, seeing Moyna return with her filled pail. 'Very good habit − drinking milk,' she added, contriving to make Moyna understand that this was an indirect comment on the evil of drinking wine. 'Or you are making curd? Kheer pudding, then? No? You don't know how to make kheer pudding?'

The next signal Mao gave was an audible one: a strange, unexpected, long drawn-out wail in the night that woke Moyna and made her shoot out of bed, ready to leap to the door. Mao himself was nowhere to be seen; he generally slipped in and out of the window which had a missing pane that Mr Bhalla had never thought to replace and now proved a convenience. Looking through it, Moyna saw, as in a dream, a feline bacchanalia in full swing on the rooftop. How had all these female felines found their way to the barsati − and to

Mao? Moyna rushed out in her nightgown to make sure the door was locked. It was. Was there a drainpipe they might have climbed? There couldn't be or Mao would have discovered it long ago. As she stood wondering, the cats crept into a corner discreetly screened by a box or two, and as she watched, the pipal tree gave a shiver. The pipal tree – of course! She stared at its massive trunk, pale in the moonlight, and the sinuous branches and twigs silvery and ashiver, and spied another insomniac – her neighbour, a few feet away, his moony face cupped in his hands as he leaned upon the ledge and gazed yearningly at her. He was close enough to speak to her but, instead, he first sighed and then began to hum. It sounded like the tune of a disgusting song to Moyna's ears, a lewd, suggestive song, an outrageous affront of a song:

'O, a girl is like a flame,
O, a girl can start a fire –'

Moyna darted back into her room and slammed the door. Its echoes rang out and for a while there was a shocked silence. But, a little later, the cats crept out to caterwaul again and all Moyna could do was wrap a pillow round her head and moan.

Although she did her best to avoid the Bhallas next morning – and usually when she left for work they were in the dining room, from which tantalising whiffs of fried dough, curried eggs and creamy tea floated out – today Mrs Bhalla was lying in wait, having her scalp massaged at that very hour. She looked up from under the tent of greying hair spread out on her shoulders and fixed her eye on the rapidly fleeing Moyna. 'Come here!' she cried. 'I'm late!' shouted Moyna from the gate. 'What is that animal on your roof?' shrieked

Mrs Bhalla, throwing off the ministering fingers of the old crone she had engaged for the service. 'Animal?' called Moyna from the other side of the gate, 'What animal?' and jumped across the ditch to the dusty road where Gurmail Singh waited for her, his autorickshaw put-putting reassuringly.

Catastrophe struck from an unexpected quarter. Returning from work the same day, Moyna climbed slowly up the stairs with a bag of fish she had stopped to buy, unlocked the door to the rooftop and went in, sighing with relief at having gained the open barsati, at seeing the pipal tree dark against the mauve and pink evening sky, wondering if there was enough water in the bucket for a wash. She let herself into her room and set about putting away her sling bag, her market bag, slipping out of her slippers, shedding the day like a worn garment, sweaty and dusty. Mao was not around but he rarely was now that he had discovered the route of the pipal tree: there was nothing she could do but hope Candy would not be waiting at the foot of it. She decided to switch on some music instead, reached out − and saw the blank space beside her bed where she kept her radio and tape recorder. It was not there.

Her first foolish reaction was to blame Mao. Could he have taken it? Then she whirled around, thinking she might have placed it elsewhere last night, or this morning, and forgotten. It was not on the kitchen table, and there was no other surface where it could be. Looking around for some corner where it might have hidden itself, she began to notice other objects were missing: her alarm clock, the little box containing the tapes, even the tin-framed mirror she had hung on the wall. What else? Flinging open the cupboard that would not lock, she began to cry as she groped on the shelves, trying to count her saris. Wiping her face with her hand, she banged it shut and ran down the stairs to the Bhallas.

They were all seated crosslegged on the bed, chins cupped in their hands, deeply absorbed in the latest episode of their favourite American soap opera (the mythological epics were aired only on Sundays, to guarantee maximum viewership). Sweetie and Pinky refused to turn their attention away from *I Love Lucy* but the elder Bhallas sensed Moyna's hysteria, turned off the TV, listened to her tearful outburst, then burst themselves, with fulsome indignation. What was she insinuating? Was she accusing *them*? Did she think *they* would go up to her barsati and haul away her miserable goods – *they*, with all these goods of their own around them . . .

Now Moyna had to deny their accusation, assure them she had never harboured such an idea, only wanted to know if they had any idea *who* it could be. *Who?* they thundered, how would they know *who?* What with Moyna's unsavoury circle of friends coming and going at all hours of the day and night, how could they tell which one had found his way to her barsati? Had they seen anyone? she begged. *Seen* anyone? Seen *who?* they roared. At this point, she wailed, 'Please call the police!' which incensed them further. They nearly exploded – even Candy, Sweetie and Pinky shrank back. Police? On their property? What was Moyna suggesting? Was she out of her mind? If the police visited their house, their immaculate, impeccable house of decency, purity and family values, what would their neighbours think, or say? Never had such a thing happened in their home, their locality, their community – till *she* had come along and brought into their midst this evil, this sin . . .

Moyna retreated. She shut the door upon the Bhallas, who were standing at the foot of the stairs and shaking their fists and shouting loud enough for all the neighbours to hear. Then she sat down on a chair under the tree, feeling as if all her strength were gone; she could not even stand. Mao reappeared, wrapping himself around and around her legs, finally leaping onto her lap and kneading it with his paws, loudly purring. She held him, sure he was telling her something, saying comforting, consoling things, and sat there till it was dark, listening to him and the pipal tree that shivered and rustled, the birds subsiding into its branches, eventually falling silent. More than any other sensation, it was homesickness she felt: she was trying to suppress the most childish urge to run and hide her head in her mother's lap, feel her mother stroking her hair. She was also suppressing the urge to write a long letter home, describing everything as it really was. She told herself it would be unforgivable to cause her parents concern. As it was, they had never felt comfortable about her living alone in the big city; every letter from them voiced their anxiety, begging her to keep her doors securely locked, never go out after dark and take good care of her health. She also knew she was trying to hold onto her pride, as she sat there, stroking and stroking Mao.

Still, Moyna knew she had to do something, and planned to tell Tara immediately. But next morning Tara had arranged to hold a 'conference', as she liked to call such a gathering, with their usual cast of reviewers. Most of them were Ritwick's friends and colleagues from the Jawaharlal Nehru University, with a sprinkling of 'outsiders' from Delhi University and the lesser colleges. This was not a regular meeting but somehow, by some kind of natural osmosis that no one quite understood, the hard core of their critics who reviewed reguarly for *Books* happened to have a free morning and came to meet Tara and

Moyna at the Coffee House in Connaught Place where they took up a long table in one corner. This was the occasion, greatly enjoyed by all, when the young lecturers and readers pleaded for the books they were desperate to have, the latest academic treatises published by the university presses at Oxford and Cambridge, Harvard and Yale, at impossible prices, and Tara and Moyna magnanimously dispensed them with the understanding that the reviewers could expect little reward other than the prized books themselves. In return, the eager young men in their handspun shirts, shaggy beards and dusty sandals plied them with small earthen mugs of coffee and all the delicacies the Coffee House had to offer – dosa, idli, vada, whatever they liked – and which harried waiters flapping dishcloths and tin trays around brought to them in regular relays. There were also some professional critics, usually older men, some really quite old, worn and grey from years of piecing together a living by writing, who looked over the books with a more practised and cynical eye and quickly reached for whatever would take the least time to read and fetch the most at the second-hand bookshops on the pavement outside.

But the customary bonhomie of the occasion which recalled their carefree student days – O careless youth! – was unexpectedly disrupted that morning by Moyna's state of agitation which she could not conceal, leading to an open confession under questioning from Tara. Theft, landlords, police – all were appalled and looked at Moyna in horror.

'Bloody lumpen proletariat!' raged the young man who always contrived to sit directly across from Moyna in order to gaze at her when he was not looking out for a book he could attack and demolish. 'Should be taught a lesson. Think they rule the world, huh? Have to be shown –'

'By whom? The polizia? Those stooges –'

This enraged the young gallant. 'If not, I'll make them. Come on, Moyna, I'll go to the police if the landlord won't –'

Moyna grew alarmed. She had here all the reaction she could have asked for but was not at all sure if she wanted to go any further, that is, go to the police about it. She had come to the office that morning hoping Tara or Raj Kumar or Mohan might offer to go with her, or at least offer symapthy and advice. Then she had found Tara bustling about, arranging to leave the office to Raj Kumar and go to the Coffee House with Moyna and a pile of books, while Raj Kumar settled down to telephone all his friends and Mohan was poring over a postcard from his sisters about a prospective bride they had found for him. She had had to hold back the matter till it had burst from her when someone merely asked, 'How's life, Moyna?' which in turn had lead to this show of outrage and gallantry.

A few minutes later Ritwick dropped in on the conference, hoping to pick up a book on medieval trade routes through the Arabian Sea that Tara had promised to keep for him. On hearing of Moyna's calamity, he insisted on accompanying her and Karan to the police station. 'Is there a justice system or is there not?' he demanded, glaring at all around the table with its coffee cups, its trays and plates of greasy fried food. 'I need to know!'

At the police station, the officer in charge sat at his desk looking uncomfortable in a khaki uniform that did not fit and had to be nudged, tugged and scratched into place constantly. Several lesser officials stood around with their nightsticks, and stared at Moyna with open mouths while the two men did all the talking. Moyna was glad not to have to speak but she did have to sign the yellow charge sheet that the officer filled out with slow deliberation, then handed to her. When she had done that, he rose from his chair and commanded his underlings to follow him to the Bhalla household.

At the gate, Moyna's courage failed. She looked around wildly in the hope of seeing Gurmail Singh with his autorickshaw ready to put-put her away from the scene, but of course he was not there and Ritwick and Karan between them silently compelled her to open the gate and lead the party in.

Only Mrs Bhalla was at home at that hour; the servant boy vanished from sight as soon as the police made their appearance. Nevertheless, the scene was awful. Or so it seemed to Moyna although, in retrospect, perhaps not as awful as it might have been. It was true that Mrs Bhalla stood at the foot of the stairs, screaming imprecations against tenants who made false accusations and brought disgrace to the homes that sheltered them, but the police merely marched past her and up the stairs, stalked around the barsati, twisting their moustaches like comic-book or cartoon cops, pointing out the sights to each other with an amused, even bemused air – Mao stretched out on the bed, blinking lazily at the intruders, the neighbours peering over the walls and ledges with open curiosity, Moyna's toilet goods arranged on the windowsill – and examined the full height and length of the pipal tree, then climbed down the stairs, and vanished. 'Complaint has been filed,' they told the indignant Ritwick and Karan. 'Investigation has been completed.'

When Moyna queued up at the Mother Dairy with her milk can next morning, she found herself standing next to a young woman she had often noticed there but never spoken to: she seemed to be a foreigner, with light brown hair pulled back and tied in a long pigtail down her back, wearing the cheapest of cotton saris and rubber slippers. Now the young woman spoke to her, unexpectedly. 'I have heard,' she said haltingly, 'you have had – theft?' Moyna nodded, and hardly dared reply, knowing everyone in the line was listening. Many did turn around at the word 'theft'. 'I too,' said the young woman sympathetically. 'I see you on roof. I, too,' she said, and after they had had their milk cans filled, they walked back together along the dusty verge of the road, and Simona told Moyna how she had employed a boy who had regularly burgled her barsati of anything she bought for it. 'But didn't you dismiss him?' Moyna asked, thinking that even she would have had the wits to do that. 'Of course,' Simona replied, 'after first time! But he had key for my barsati, came back and thieved again, and again. Now I have nothing left, nothing,' she added, with a joyful smile. 'And the police –?' 'Oh, they caught him – again, and again. But always they had to let him go because he said he was twelve years old! Too young for gaol.' Simona shrugged. 'Still he is twelve. He does not grow any older. So he can be thief for longer.'

This gave Moyna so much food for thought that she walked along in silence, and almost forgot to ask Simona her name or address. When she did, it turned out that Simona was one of her neighbours, only too discreet to hang over her ledge and spy on Moyna like the others. Now she promised to wave and call when she saw Moyna out on her rooftop. 'You have most beautiful tree,' she said on parting, and Moyna glowed till it struck her it could be the reason why she stayed on with the Bhallas, and if that would not be considered foolishness by anyone but Simona.

The next day Tara and Ritwick came to visit. They stalked around the rooftop, peering through every possible loophole through which the burglar might re-enter. The trouble was that he probably had a key to the door and could let himself in whenever Moyna left: it was unlikely he risked climbing the great tree in the backyard.

'This place is just not secure, Moyna. You've got to ask your landlord to make it secure. Fence in the entire outer wall –'

'Ask Mr Bhalla?' Moyna croaked.

Lately whenever Moyna passed through the Bhalla home she felt she needed protective clothing. Mr Bhalla's jowls seemed set in a permanent scowl like a thunder cloud (the fact that he rarely shaved and his jaws were always blue added to the illusion) while Mrs Bhalla would plant herself in a central location, her eyes following Moyna down to the gate or up the stairs as if she suspected Moyna herself of the theft. Her mutterings implied as much – 'These girls, these days, think they can go to work, live alone – huh! Can't even take care of their own belongings!' Did she actually say these words, or was Moyna imagining them? She felt them creep over her back, across her neck, like spiders settling there.

As for their servant boy, after her conversation with Simona, Moyna was certain she sensed an extra insouciance to his manner. He had always watched her with open, unconcealed curiosity, but now she felt he gave his hips an insulting swing, twitched his filthy kitchen duster over his shoulder with a flick, and pursed his lips to whistle a bar from some Bombay film tune although that was surely not fitting in a servant boy, even if employed in a household like the Bhallas'. When she passed the open kitchen door one day and he cocked an eyebrow at her and sang:

'With blouse cut low, with hair cut short,
This memsahib so fine —'

she decided to complain to the Bhallas, but discovered she had
chosen a bad moment: that very morning, while she was at
work, Mao had slithered down the tree trunk to the Bhallas'
compound and been pounced upon by Candy, with Sweetie
and Pinky in hot pursuit. Mao had somehow escaped from all
three, but Moyna's secret of owning what the Bhallas
insultingly called a 'billa', a tom, had been uncovered. Rising
to her feet, Mrs Bhalla launched into a tirade about lying
tenants who neglected to inform their landlords of their pets
that would never have been permitted into their own pristine
homes. Moyna, already incensed by the servant boy's
behaviour and now by his employers', stood her ground
stoutly and replied, 'Then do you want me to leave?' half
hoping the reply would free her of them. But Mrs Bhalla
retreated promptly — she knew to a whisker's breadth how far
she could go as a landlady — claiming she could hear the
telephone ringing. That evening she sent Pinky and Sweetie
upstairs to ask if Moyna would like to come down and watch a
rerun of the old film classic Awaara with them. Moyna told
them she had a cold.

It was not untrue. The change of season had affected Moyna
as it had practically every other citizen of Delhi. Still listless
from the heat during the day, at night she found herself
shivering under her cotton quilt in the barsati: the window-
pane had never been replaced and allowed a chill blast of
wintry air in.

She was sniffling over her desk at the office one morning
with her head in her hands, trying to correct proofs, only half-

listening to Tara complain of her mother-in-law's unreasonable and ungenerous reaction to Tara and Ritwick's staying out at the cinema late last night, when a visitor appeared at the door, demanding to see the editor. Tara's tirade was cut short, she hastily tossed her nail file into a drawer, pulled a page of proofs from Moyna's desk, and lifted an editorial expression to a man whose face appeared to be made entirely out of bristling hair and gleaming teeth, although he did wear thick, black-framed glasses and a silk scarf as well, tucked into the v-neck of a purple sweater.

'What can I do for you?' Tara had barely asked when she began to regret it.

The visitor was the author of a collection of short stories in Hindi that had been reviewed by Karan in the last issue. He had a copy of it rolled up in his hand. He spread it out before them, asking if they, as editors, had paid attention to what they were printing in a journal that at one time had had a distinguished reputation but now was nothing but a rag in the filthy hands of reviewers like the one who signed himself KK. Did they know who he was talking about?

Moyna got up and came across to glance at the review together with Tara, out of a sense of loyalty to her and an awareness of threat, as the author of the short stories jabbed his finger at one line, then another – 'so devoid of imagination that Sri Awasthi has had to borrow from sources such as *The Sound of Music* and –' 'in language that would get a sixth standard student in trouble with his teacher –' 'situations so absurd that he can hardly expect his readers to take them any more seriously than the nightly soap opera on TV –' 'characters cut out of cardboard and pasted onto the page with Sri Awasthi's stunning lack of subtlety –'

Tara recovered her poise before Moyna could. Snatching

the journal out of the visitor's hands, she held it out of his reach. 'We choose our reviewers for their standing in the academic world. Every one of them is an authority on –'

'Authority? What authority? This dog – he claims he is an authority on Hindi literature?' ranted the man, snatching the journal back from Tara. 'It is a scandal – such a standard of reviewing is a scandal. It must not go unnoticed – or unpunished. Where is this man? I would like to see him. I should like to know –'

'If you have any complaint, you can make it in writing,' Tara told him. She was, Moyna could see, as good a fighter as she had always claimed.

'Make it in writing? If I make it, will you publish it? If I put in writing what I think of your journal, your name will be –'

'Mr Awasthi,' Tara said, using his name as if she remembered it with difficulty, and managing to mispronounce it, 'there is no need to be so insulting.'

'If that is so, then why have I been insulted? I am a member of Sahitya Akademi. I am author of forty volumes of short stories, one of autobiography, seven books of travel, and also of essays. I am award-winning. I am invited by universities in foreign countries. My name is known in all Hindi-speaking areas –'

Mohan suddenly strode in; he had been standing in the doorway with Raj Kumar but now entered the room to stand beside Tara and Moyna. He was enjoying this; it was the first drama to take place in the office. Plucking the journal out of Mr Awasthi's hands, he tossed it on the desk with a contemptuous gesture. 'The editor is not responsible for the reviewer's views,' he announced, which it had not occurred to the two women to say.

This was not very original but Mr Awasthi's face turned a

dangerously purple colour, not unlike the sweater he wore. But now Mohan had him by the elbow and was guiding him out of the door. Tara and Moyna fell back into their chairs, pushing their hair away from their flushed faces. Tara, lighting a cigarette with shaking hands, said, 'Did you *hear* Mohan? Did you *see* how he got him out?'

That visit proved to be a prelude to an entire winter in which the battle raged. Mr Awasthi's rebuttal was printed in the next issue, followed by Karan's still more scurrilous response – he worked in an attack on the Hindi-speaking 'cow belt' which proved a starting point for a whole new series of entertaining insults – and their days at the office were enlivened by visits from either one or other, each intent on getting the 'editor's ear' (in the case of Karan, it was mostly the Assistant Editor's ear he tried to get). Even Bose Sahib wrote from Calcutta and implored Tara to close the correspondence on the matter (he thought mention of the 'cow belt' particularly deplorable and unparliamentary). He added some disquieting remarks that Tara relayed to Moyna gloomily. 'He says the journal is still in the red, and he may not be able to go on publishing it if it fails to make money. Never thought Bose Sahib would consider *Books* as if it were a commercial enterprise. Ritwick says it is clear capitalism has killed Marxism in Calcutta if even Bose Sahib talks like an industrialist.'

'Oh Tara,' Moyna said in dismay. It was not just that Bose Sahib was something of an icon in their circle but it also shook her confidence in her ability to be a career woman in Delhi. What would happen if she lost her job? What if she did not find another employer? Would she lose her barsati? And return to her parents' home? Back where she started from? She began to sniffle.

Her cold, which had been growing worse for weeks, burgeoned into full-scale flu. After going downstairs to send Gurmail Singh away in his autorickshaw, she went back to bed, pulling the quilt over her ears. Mao, sympathetic or, perhaps, delighted at this development, crept in beside her. She drifted in and out of sleep, and her sleep was always crowded with thoughts of office life. Behind closed lids, she continued to see the journal's columns before her, requiring her to proofread:

Sir — Sri Ritwick Misra has reviewed Sri Nirad Chaudhuri's biography of Max Müller without proving his credentials for doing so. Has Sri Misra any knowledge of Max Müller's native tongue? Has Sri Chaudhuri? If not, can we believe all the necessary documents have been studied without which no scholar can trust, etc., Yrs truly, B. Chattopadhyay, Asansol, W. Bengal.

Sir — May I compliment you on your discovery of a true genius, i.e Srimati Devika Bijlinai, whose poem, *Lover, lover*, is a work of poetic excellence. I hope you will continue to publish the work of this lovable poetess. Kindly convey my humble respects to her. Also publish photograph of same in next issue. Yrs truly, A. Reddy, Begumpet, Hyderabad, A.P.

It was in this state that Raj Kumar found her when he came in with a message from Tara saying, 'Why won't you get yourself a phone, Moyna, and tell us when you're not coming to work? Just when the new issue is ready to go to press —' and ending 'Shall I bring over a doctor this evening?'

Moyna was not sure what to do with Raj Kumar but was grateful for his obvious concern and felt she could not send him straight back to the office. 'Can I make you a cup of tea, Raj Kumar?' she asked hoarsely. 'I'll have some, too.'

Raj Kumar perched on the edge of her straight-backed chair. He planted his hands on his knees, and studied every object in the room with the same deep interest while Moyna boiled water in a pan and got out the earthen mugs to make tea.

'No TV?' he asked finally.

She shook her head and put a few biscuits on a plate to offer him. He ate one with great solemnity, as if considering its qualities, then asked, 'Who is doing the cooking?' She admitted she did her own, wondering who he imagined would perform such chores for her. 'Ah, that is why you are never bringing lunch from home,' he said, with pity. She agreed it was. He of course had a wife to fill a tiffin container's three or four compartments to bursting with freshly cooked, still warm food. He asked for more details of her domestic existence. As Moyna told him of her regimen of rising to store water at five, then queueing for milk at six, and the shopping she did at the market on her way home with the essential stop at the fish shop for Mao's diet, Raj Kumar's eyes widened. He was too polite to say anything but when he had finished his tea and biscuits and rose to go, he said in a voice of true concern, 'Please lock door safely. Not safe to live alone like this.' She assured him she would.

At the door he turned to say, 'Also, you should purchase TV set,' with great earnestness. 'TV set is good company,' he explained, 'like friend.'

Going back to bed after shutting and locking the door behind him, she did feel friendless – but not convinced that she wanted a TV in place of one. And no sooner had she closed her eyes than the lines of print began to unroll again:

Sir – It is a great disappointment that you continue to harbour a reviewer such as KK who has a clear bias against one of the great languages of our motherland. Because he is reviewing for an English-language journal in the capital, does he think he has the right to spurn the literature composed in the vernacular? This attitude is as despicable as the sight of seeing mother's milk rejected for sake of foreign liquor. Yrs truly, C. Bhanot, Pataliputra Colony, Bihar.

Sir – The monthly arrival of *Books* is greatly looked forward to by my immediate family. I regret that you choose to include in it such filth as Srimati Devika Bijliani's poem, *Lover, lover.* This is not what we expect to find in decent family magazine. Kindly refrain from publishing offensive matter of sexual nature and return to former family status. Yrs truly, D. Ramanathan, Trivandrum, Kerala.

Simona, not having seen Moyna in the milk queue for days, came to visit. She brought with her a gift that touched Moyna deeply – fish tails and heads wrapped in newspaper for Mao's dinner. Simona explained, 'I saw you are not getting milk so I know that cat is not getting fish.' She sat crosslegged on Moyna's bed, tucking her cotton sari around her shoulders, and told Moyna that she herself had been sick – 'for many, many days. Months, perhaps. Hep-a-ti-tis. You have hep-a-ti-tis?' 'Oh no,' Moyna denied it vigorously, 'only flu,' and was afraid to think now that she might lie alone in the barsati for so long, sick, away from home. 'And you are so far from home,' she said to Simona with sudden sympathy, and wondered what could keep the young woman here, ageing before her eyes into a pale, drawn invalid. But Simona put on her rapt expression, one that often overtook her even in the most inconvenient places – passing the garbage heap behind the marketplace, for instance, or seeing a beggar approach – and told Moyna joyfully, 'This is my home. It is where my guru lives, you see.' Moyna cowered under her quilt: she did not feel strong enough for such revelations. 'Please make yourself tea,' she croaked, and broke into a paroxysm of coughs.

Having received a letter in which Moyna mentioned that she had flu, Moyna's mother arrived. Moyna was actually on her way to recovery by then and many of the remedies her mother brought with her, the special teas and balms and syrups, were no longer needed, but evidently much else was. Putting her hand into the containers on Moyna's kitchen shelf, her mother was shocked to find less than a handful of rice, of lentils. 'You are starving!' she exclaimed, as horrified at herself as her daughter, 'and we did not know!' 'Do I look as if I'm starving?' Moyna asked, but she could not stop her mother from shopping and cooking and storing food in a storm of energy and activity in the barsati, which was now bathed in mild sunlight and at its most livable in Delhi's pleasant winter.

Mrs Bhalla downstairs roused herself too, and began to cook and send treats upstairs, either with the servant boy or with Pinky or Sweetie, little jars of pickles she had put up, or metal trays with sweets she had made, dissolving in pools of oil and reeking of rose water, or covered pots containing specialities known only to Mrs Bhalla and the village that was once her home.

'How kind she is,' Moyna's mother exclaimed, accepting these gifts. 'How lucky you are to have found such a landlady, Moyna.'

Nothing Moyna told her could completely alter her mother's impression. 'She's just trying to fool you,' she cried. 'She *wants* you to think she's a nice person.'

She glowered at Mrs Bhalla whenever she passed her on the veranda, but Mrs Bhalla now called out to her with great sweetness, 'How is your mother, Moyna? Please ask her to come and visit me.'

'I don't know why you both like each other so much,' Moyna said darkly, on conveying this message.

'We are both mothers, that is why,' her mother replied with what Moyna now found an indigestible sweetness. It was this motherliness she had missed and longed for but now she found it superfluous. Her barsati no longer looked as it had in the days of penury, austerity and minimalism. Her mother had bought curtains, cushions, filled every available space with kitchen gadgets, foods, whatever comfort she could think of. Now Moyna found she was no longer used to comfort, that it annoyed and irritated her. Picking up Mao and a book, she would retreat to the rooftop while her mother bustled about in the crowded room, clattering and humming and enjoying herself. She leaned over the ledge and stared moodily into the quaking leaves of the pipal tree and the hazy winter light that filtered through. Downstairs, in the Bhallas' brightly lit kitchen, she could see the Bhallas' servant boy, rolling out chapatis for their dinner. He had music on to entertain him while he worked, and Moyna listened too. She was enjoying its somewhat melancholy and dirge-like tone when she started in recognition: was that not Joan Baez singing? And was it not one of her own tapes? She stiffened and bent over the ledge, trying to look past the pipal leaves to get a clearer picture of what was on the kitchen counter below. But she did not really need to look, she could hear clearly enough, and it made her roll her hands into fists and pound on the ledge with frustration.

While her instinct was to run and tell her mother, then run down and inform Mrs Bhalla and demand her belongings back, she found herself silent. Letting her mother pile a spinach curry and lentils on her plate at dinner, she kept quiet: she knew it would be unwise to tell her mother that she lived amongst thieves. How then could she declare to her that she intended to remain here with them, not return to family and home, comfort and care?

'What are you thinking, Moyna?' her mother asked impatiently. 'Why don't you eat?'

Fortunately, her mother could not stay long. Unfortunately, when Moyna returned with relief to her own routine, she found Tara at the office consumed by the same housemaking fervour. This was not at all customary where Tara was concerned. Tara had taken the job at *Books* to escape from housewifeliness, as her mother-in-law so cannily suspected – and now she confounded Moyna by talking incessantly of real estate, bank loans, co-ops . . . true, not housekeeping matters exactly, but just as boring to Moyna who had plunged into the next issue which had yet another blistering attack by Karan on the Hindi author's newest offering. Tara was hardly around to see to it; she was either on the telephone, earnestly discussing finances with Ritwick, or, with her handbag slung over her shoulder and her dark glasses on, was off to visit yet another co-op.

'Why are you doing this?' Moyna protested. 'You *have* a nice house to live in. I mean,' she added hastily, seeing Tara's expression, 'I know it's the Dragon Lady's, but still, it *is* nice and you don't pay for it —' She refrained from mentioning the free babysitting service it provided.

'You don't understand. You're too young. At our age, we need our own place,' Tara explained loftily.

In her concern for this nest for the future, Tara seemed strangely unaffected by the letter they received from Bose Sahib, announcing his decision to close the magazine. He was planning to start another, he added, this time about development projects in rural areas — were Tara and Moyna interested in working for it? Tara would not even consider it: she was settling into this nest she had found, she was not going to go touring the hinterland, she would turn down the offer. Moyna was pale with dismay and disbelief; she begged Tara not to speak so loudly, to come down to the sweet shop below where they could discuss it over a cup of tea without Mohan and Raj Kumar overhearing. 'It will be such a shock to them,' she explained to Tara. But Tara did not see any cause for shock: 'Mohan is looking for a job in hotels anyway, or a travel agency,' she said. 'What?' asked Moyna. Why had she not been told the world of *Books* was coming unravelled around her? Had she been so immersed in the wretched business of barsati living to ignore far more important matters? What about all the book reviewers and their supply of foreign books being cut short? She sat at the small tin-topped table with Tara, not able to swallow her tea, and pleaded with her to reconsider. 'But why?' Tara asked, her eyes looking into the distance where her dream house waited for her like a mirage in the desert outside Delhi. 'I'm not married to *Books*, or to Bose Sahib. Let them go to hell. I'm not going to go around looking at weaving centres and dairy farms for Bose Sahib!'

Moyna bit her lip. It was certainly not what she had come to Delhi for, nor was it what she had expected to do with her life. But she had grown used to the two-roomed office with its bamboo shutters, Raj Kumar sitting in a corner and tying up book parcels, Mohan enjoying his bun omelette and samosas at his desk. She had even grown used, if that was what resignation could be called, to the barsati, although when the year's lease was up, she would be free to rent another: there were almost as many barsatis in Delhi as there were top-floor flats. She turned the teaspoon over and over in her hands, considering all the possibilities, weighing the pros and cons, till Tara snatched it out of her hand. 'Stop fidgeting, Moyna. Just *decide*,' she snapped, tossing back her hair with all the authority of someone who had done just that.

It was too difficult, too weighty a decision to be made in a moment, over a cup of tea. Moyna went back and forth between the office and the barsati, sick with anxiety. Only occasionally and momentarily could she forget the problem: when Gurmail Singh told her with pride that his daughter had passed the entrance test to the Loreto Convent, ensuring a fine future for her and leaving him only to worry about his less promising son; or when she received an invitation to a film show at the British Council to be followed by a reception, placing her on a rung above those who went there only for the air conditioning and the newspapers. Then she would fall to brooding again and sit crosslegged on her bed, stroking Mao and turning the matter over in her mind.

It was when she was in such a state that a letter arrived from her mother. She opened it listlessly, knowing in advance what it would contain — advice on how to run her household, how to cook a specially strengthening stew, an offer of monetary help, pleas to return home, her father's message that she should consider studying for a higher degree before embarking on a career – and she glanced at it cursorily: her mother did not understand even now the attraction of living, alone, in Delhi, and could think of it only as a poor substitute for living at home.

But at the bottom of this letter, her mother had added, craftily:

Our neighbours have invited us to a welcome party next week; their son Arun is returning from the United States. He has taken a degree in geology and is expected to find a suitable job in the field. I am sure he would be pleased to meet you again. If you are planning a visit soon, we shall ask him over for a meal. I know his family is very keen . . .

Mao gave a leap off the bed as Moyna flung herself backwards, at the same time throwing the letter into the air with a shout of laughter. She rolled her head about on the pillow, spluttering, 'Oh, Mama – re-a-ll-y, Mama!' Mao had not seen such behaviour in a long time. He sat by the door and watched her, his paws primly together, his tail wrapped around him, disapproving. It was clear he thought she had gone crazy. Even he, with his fine senses, could not know that the letter made up Moyna's mind for her. She was free, she was determined, she had made her decision, and she sat up, laughing.

In the kitchen below, the Bhallas' servant boy turned up the music and sang along with it.